Thirty Pieces

Also by Garry Kinnane

George Johnston: A Biography
Colin Colahan: A Portrait.
Sunlight: The Shadowed Days Trilogy
Shadowed Days
Fare Thee Well, Hoddle Grid
Time of Arrival

GARRY KINNANE

Thirty Pieces

Stories and Poems

rainshadow

ISBN: (paperback) 978-1-7637356-4-4
ISBN (hardback) 978-1-7637356-3-7

Published by rainshadow, an imprint of Clouds of Magellan Press, Melbourne
www.cloudsofmagellanpress.net.

Design: Gordon Thompson
Cover image: Zen Summer, on Unsplash

Contents

Acknowledgements

Introduction

Except that A.D. Hope has already beaten me to the title, I might easily have called this volume of stories and poems 'a late picking'; or some such. And this is because, although it is my first book of creative work, the contents have almost all been written since my retirement from university lecturing in 2004. Now 87, I certainly don't qualify for any young writers' awards, and yet I do feel like a beginner in important ways. It would be nice to think that there is a freshness in my approach that comes, not from any Writing Course formulas, but from my interest in the life going on around me. One of my favourite pieces of advice came from Sir Philip Sidney's Muse, who told him to leave 'learning' behind, and 'Fool… look in thy heart and write'. Of course, it's not as easy as the Muse would imply, and in any case I'm sure that 'creativity' is as learned as scholarship. And yet I did find the material for all these pieces in my 'heart', which is only another way of saying from my experience, real and imagined.

There is a range of different themes explored in these pieces; several are concerned with ageing, ill-health, dependence, friendship and especially memory – the distant as well as the recent past and how it stays with us into old age. Retirement has given me time to observe my peers, time to reflect on the world of seniority and its hazards, but also time to relive the challenges of youth and to recall its mistakes. I don't know whether old age provides wisdom, but it certainly provides stories, if only we can recall them. And if not, we can make them up. Here are thirty, some in prose, some in verse, that came to me in one way or another.

Garry Kinnane
Waurn Ponds
September 2025

Stories

Friday

Iris Edmonds wakes as early as 5.30 these mornings, preoccupied with the clutter of tasks, memories and fantasies jumbling through her head – yesterday's news on the Middle East, the latest road fatality, a brochure that came in the post advertising an enticing educational tour of Italy, the recollection of a beautiful moment watching ice-skaters with her husband Peter in New York's Central Park; it takes mental concentration to sort out the immediate demands from those that can be pushed into the background. And this morning the book group is coming to the house. The Ian McEwan novel. Which she has barely started.

She is aware of the breathing beside her as Peter hunches into the blankets in heavy sleep. He won't stir until about 8 o'clock, and then her thinking time will be over and she will have to get down to practical matters. She can't let him shower on his own now; even after a handrail was fitted and a shower seat bought he still fell getting out, cracked his head on the bath edge. Yet another hospital visit. So she undresses and gets in with him now, washes his hair and privates, tries not to let the fact of their spotted, wrinkled bodies depress her. Actually, he's still a handsome man, even in his late 70s; the ravages of age have been kinder to him than to her. She can't bear to look at herself in the mirror.

He can dress himself, but he dithers so long over it that she has now even taken charge of that rather than leave him sitting on the bed in a mire of indecision all morning; she chooses his dark grey trousers and the pink shirt she bought him for Christmas last year, and would have put him in his navy pullover, but he insists on the black 'hoodie'. It's the one feature of current dress style amongst younger males that he has taken to; he detests jeans and synthetic 'jogger' shoes, insisting on traditional leather at all times, but his hands are so unsteady now that Iris always has to do up the laces.

She will just have time to get his breakfast and get back from the shops before the book group starts at 10 o'clock. This afternoon she has washing to put out, weather permitting, and the floors need doing. She wishes the home help the council has scheduled were available immediately, but the wait for that is still over a year. Sometime next week – Thursday – the car goes in for a service. And she needs to take Peter to a dental appointment Wednesday. He complains that they have taken away his licence, but the fact is he is not safe to drive any more, not since he backed over the garbage bin last year and ended in the flower bed. God, it feels she has more to do now than at any previous time in her life.

It is late January, and the forecast is for the weekend to warm up, so after breakfast she gives the garden some water. She is dismayed by the growth of weeds in amongst the roses, the way thistles are pushing through the azaleas, the kangaroo paws looking colourless and falling over. She struggles to keep up with the garden. It was always Peter's thing. He planted and tended the vegetables, kept the flower beds weeded; she was never enthusiastic. But he doesn't do any of that now; it's all he can do to stay awake between meals. He spends his time gazing out of the lounge room window as if he can see something interesting, but she knows he can't. He is day-dreaming, or whatever his mental state could be called; a closed book. She doesn't like to leave him for long, tries to be as quick as she can doing the shopping.

Her friends in the book group provide the one regular moment of enjoyment of the week. Their enthusiastic chat when they arrive each Friday is like food to a starving waif. As always, it takes them twenty minutes or so before they get down to discussing the book; they have much to catch up on since last week – medical reportage mostly, and the doings of grandchildren, which most of them have. Jane is saying that she and Dulcie and another friend, not in the book group, are going off after lunch to spend the weekend at a music festival in Daylesford; this evening it is scenes from operas – *Carmen, Rigoletto, La Traviata,* with some well-known singers. Everyone is excited for them. The aroma of coffee floods the room while they chat, cups in hand, biscuits at the ready. Iris thinks, 'What a lovely group they are'.

Peter comes into the room while they talk, a grey ghost staggering with the help of a stick, sits himself in an easy chair a distance away from the group. He won't, indeed can't, participate. He just gazes around and smiles. Eventually, he will fall asleep. Dulcie is leading the discussion today; the novel about a youth who is seduced by his music teacher. Iris hasn't found time to finish it, but Dulcie's talk gives her a good overall sense of the story. Their discussion turns to the rights and wrongs of sex between people of very different ages. Almost against her will Iris finds herself taking a somewhat libertarian view; the others all deplore the idea of a teacher seducing a pupil, but Iris thinks this is too formulaic, and that it is possible to imagine a situation where it is good for both parties. 'Surely it depends on the specifics,' she says, 'the people, their circumstances, the way the affair is conducted. I'm sure many happy marriages have resulted from an illicit relationship'. She saw that her friends were shocked by this view, and their emphatic rejection worries her; has she gone too far? But they are kind to her, and eventually laugh it off as one of those daring but jokey comments they all make from time to time.

At the end of the discussion Barbara sees that the general stirring has woken Peter, and goes over to speak with him. Watching this, Iris is reminded how attractive he has always been to women and that even now she can see that the interest Barbara shows is partly that. When Barbara asks how he is feeling, placing a mottled white hand on the arm of his pullover, he breaks out in a croaky voice, 'Alright I suppose. It's the hallucinations that are the worst…'

'What sort of hallucinations?'

'The other morning… there are two pictures in the bedroom. They rose up off the floor and just went…. like that (gesturing with both hands)… and…'

Barbara finishes the sentence for him, 'Hung themselves on the wall?'

'Yes. Yes, exactly,' he nods with a vacant grin.

Barbara replies that he should enjoy such visions. 'Most of us never experience anything so exciting,' she adds, but Peter doesn't seem to grasp her point, and simply nods and smiles.

On her way out Dulcie draws Iris aside. 'You know you should be thinking of a nursing home for Peter; he's just too much work for you. And you need to be able to get out of the house, get out from under him, sometimes. In fact I have a friend who has just gone into that new one down south, off the highway, and she just loves it there. I could give you the details.'

'I know, the thought has crossed my mind over and over, but it would hurt him. He has always said, 'I'd rather jump off a bridge than end up in one of those places', so I don't think I could do it to him. Thanks anyway.'

Preparing ham and pickle sandwiches for his lunch, Iris tries to remember exactly when she found out about his affair. Yes, around the time they moved to the house in Malvern – a step up for them a year or so after he became general manager of the company. He'd been in insurance since he left school, had worked his way up through claims, then underwriting, and finally, in his fifties, found his niche in management. Once there was no-one above him he had unchallengeable freedom to come and go as he wished, and was now 'entitled to a personal secretary', he proudly told Iris. It was when she took his grey suit for dry cleaning, went through the pockets and found a receipt from a city hotel for a double room. The booking was in the name of 'Mr and Mrs Peter Edmonds' but Iris knew damn well she'd never been anywhere near that hotel. She checked the date, and it was a Friday. He had often worked late on Fridays, or so he said, 'clearing a backlog of correspondence'. So she waited until the next time he announced it, and guessing he would use the same hotel, took an afternoon tram in to the city to see for herself. She'd had to wait almost two hours in the window seat of a cafe directly opposite the hotel, pretending to read a book but constantly eyeing the hotel entrance, until on her third cup of coffee she saw his familiar grey-suited figure walk quickly up the sloping footpath and into the hotel. It was around four-fifteen, so he was leaving himself plenty of time for his little *liaison*. The fact that he was alone confirmed Iris' suspicions – that he did not want to be seen in the street with the woman in case they were recognised. She waited, anxious, fearing; she had met Peter's secretary, a slim thirty-something blonde, at the last Christmas party. They'd talked on the phone when Peter was home sick, when Iris had sensed the voice of a cool keeper-of-confidences type; not a sharer. Several women passed through the hotel entrance alone, but only one of them qualified: a tall, hatless blonde wearing a blue coat against the July weather. It was her. This was enough. Iris went home, made dinner, put Peter's in the oven under a foil cover, and watched television until he came in. But she said nothing to him. And it wasn't the only time; obviously it became a routine, and for the next couple of years he continued to 'work overtime' on Fridays, giving nothing away. She never played the detective again, and never confronted him with what she knew. And then one day it stopped; he didn't work overtime again, and when she asked him why, he simply said, 'No need; everything is under control.' In all these years she kept quiet about it; and now she wonders why she did. Why had she allowed him to get away with it?

Sitting at the lunch table opposite Peter now, the thought strikes her that, when it came down to it, her life has been some sort of failure. Her career as a primary school teacher never amounted to much; going part-time when the children were growing up meant she was never in the running for senior positions. And she had bad luck with several schools – never found a happy one, or a sympathetic principal. But she was the first to admit, the fault was her own. She was not cut out for teaching, and should never have stayed in it. Better to have had a job that enabled her to get about; the people she most envied were those travellers – consultants or whatever – who visited clients in towns, took them to dinner, gave talks to businesses, drove around the countryside, each day a different place. She does not regret her family: she loves her children, takes some pride in having raised them to lead successful lives of their own, and dotes on her grandchildren; every Sunday they come for dinner. She loves Peter, too, despite his betrayals. He is, was, a good man, a kind man. Of course they'd had their differences over the years, but he was never mean or violent or anything like that. And the sex had mostly been good; he took it seriously, took her seriously. Perhaps that had been the source of the problem: maybe he wanted more than she could give him. But they never discussed it; sex was just one of those things you took for granted, it was a good or not so good habit that you just did, but you didn't talk about it. She wishes now she had. People do now, the young ones. But her generation was brought up differently. Even finding the right words was difficult; what could they call it? 'making love' is a bit affected; 'fucking' sounds coarse. No wonder some couples invent their own language. She read once that Gertrude Stein and Alice Toklas did that: they called their orgasms 'cows'!

'Is there any cheese?' says Peter, who has finished his sandwiches quickly and is noisily sipping his tea. She gets out the biscuits and cheddar, cuts slices and places them on his plate; again he wolfs them down, in silence, without acknowledgement. A closed book.

Of course, it is all too late now. What would she have asked him? 'Why did you do it?'

Well it was bloody-well obvious why he did, wasn't it: because he could. Because she was younger and more beautiful than me? No doubt. Men can't resist that. The flattery. The feeling of power. The real puzzle is why the women do it; same reasons? Maybe. Anyway, what's the point of being a young and beautiful woman if you don't make use of it? And would it have made any difference if they had talked about it? What really matters is that, yes, it was a betrayal, and even keeping it to himself was in his own interests, and that it pains her to think about it, but it is all too late to change. And against that she has to admit he was in other respects a good husband, a provider, and their life together had been comfortable enough. It's just that she would have liked to have found more satisfaction, more purpose, in her own activities; more than a wife, more than a mother, more than a bored schoolteacher.

It takes a moment to sink in, but the crash from the direction of the lounge room is in itself a call to action. She hears Peter half-groan-half-laugh, and dashes in to find him sprawled on the floor entangled in a metal occasional table, and struggling to get up. She rushes to him, and they spend the next minutes in a farcical wrestling act to get him at least seated. But he is too heavy. She helps to roll him onto his stomach, and from there to get his legs tucked up enough to gain leverage. With effort she gets him into a kneeling position, and then by a hauling movement they somehow get him onto the sofa. Peter laughs the whole time, as if it has been a mischievously organised game, rather than the shambles it clearly and humiliatingly is.

'What-the-hell-were-you-trying-to-do?' she demands, every word furiously emphasised.

'Ah, yes,' he earnestly replies, 'I wanted to stop that table from flying out of the window…'

'It's impossible. I don't know what I'm going to do with you, you damn fool: I can't leave you alone for two minutes without you…'

She hates this angry tone in her voice, which has only recently become evident; it is not like her at all, but sometimes, just as now, she can't help it. Patience is slowly ebbing from her, like youth, like time, like control of her life, like happiness. She is draining away.

Afterwards she ascertains that he seems to have bruised his ribs, and certainly has a large purple bruise on one hip, which she treats with Voltaren. She might have to take him to the doctor's tomorrow, if he doesn't seem better. Though it is still afternoon, she helps him on with his pajamas and settles him to bed. Later, she takes his dinner in to him on a tray, and then leaves him to settle and sleep. After the TV news, a documentary comes on SBS about Renaissance Italy; it completely absorbs her. When it's over she isn't in the mood to watch anything else, and digs out the brochure on the Italian tour that came through the post. Jane and Dulcie in Daylesford come to mind, and whether such a tour is something that might interest them; they've often talked about an overseas trip. An impulse comes to her; it is only 10.15, and she has Dulcie's mobile number. She takes up her own phone and calls; it rings only twice and Dulcie answers. They exchange greetings, and she asks what she and Jane are up to.

'Just had a lovely dinner at a local pub,' she says. 'And the concert was excellent; I'll tell you all about it when we get back.'

'Listen Dulce,' Iris says, 'I won't keep you, but I was just wondering: do you have the name of that nursing home you mentioned this morning?'

Iris writes down the name and, after a little more chat, rings off. She goes into the bedroom and checks on Peter, who is fast asleep propped up on pillows, his head thrown back and his mouth open, prompting Iris to think of those dark, cavernous catacombs that she learnt about at school. She takes up his dinner tray, turns out his table light, and goes back to the kitchen. She thinks she will sleep in the spare room tonight, as she picks up the travel brochure and reads it through yet one more time. Tomorrow, although it's Saturday, she will call the nursing home.

Seeing Margaret

It wasn't often Kendrick went to the shopping Mall alone. Mostly he went with his wife, but since she had been going to her regular lunch with her book group every Friday, and never got back before mid-afternoon, it meant that he always spent the day on his own. This particular Friday he'd noticed when taking his morning cocktail of drugs that he'd run out of his Fosinopril tablets, and needed to get to the Mall pharmacy without delay. On the ten-minute drive he found himself in an unusually happy mood – it was a beautiful autumn day, there was a lovely rendering of the Mozart piano concerto no. 21 on the radio, and for some reason the sparse traffic seemed pleasantly free of aggressive drivers.

Even walking through the broad corridor of the Waurn Ponds Mall was not as irritating as he'd anticipated. Supermarkets notwithstanding, these busy Malls are sociable places, keeping alive something of the days when people mostly walked the public footpaths to their shops, greeted their neighbours and patronized the tea-shops in the arcades, and generally made shopping into a pleasant social event. Similarly, in a Mall folks stand a pretty good chance of bumping into a friend or neighbour, just as they would have done in the streets many years ago. And today the place was less crowded, less noisy, and there seemed to be fewer screaming kids than usual. A white-coated woman at a little stall offered him a taste of something he didn't quite catch the name of; he took it and ate it and walked on without quite knowing what it was. Sausage? Dumpling? Cake? Could have been any of those.

The chemist took his prescription and gave him the choice either to wait or to come back in ten minutes; he waited, clutching the number provided. Another person was standing nearby, a woman also in line for a prescription. She threw a glance in his direction, then settled back to her unseeing gaze, cast directly in front of her. This freed him to take a look at her – about his own age, shortish, frizzed-out blonde hair with grey streaks, a thickening but not fat body showing through her open coat, fawn-coloured. Something of a Jackie Weaver about her attractively tough face. And then gradually its features began to seem familiar. Had he seen her on television perhaps? Or at the U3A centre? No, it wasn't either of these. It was a memory, not from any recent experience, but the distant past. Working at it with his imagination he tried to pare away the changes to her mouth, her jaw, the nose, the flesh and lines wrought by the passing years, searching for a younger structure within her features. The eyes would clinch it, if he could see her eyes, but at this moment they were still looking down, and shielded by her eyelids. He had once written about those eyes – 'lachrymal blue' – he wrote, and how they protruded slightly, like little glass domes. Could it be? Excitement took hold of him. My god, this *could* be her; checking over the features, he could see nothing that made it impossible. *Margaret*. Over fifty years ago! He was sixteen when he last saw her.

Now that the idea had caught him, the need to be certain became irresistible. But could he just go up and ask her? It would be risking an embarrassing scene to do it here, in public. You need care these days in approaching women you don't know, and who don't know you. The leap from enquiry to harassment has considerably shortened, and the chasm of shame deeper and more inescapable than ever before. He waited, unsure.

The chemist came to the counter carrying a little basket of medicines and called out the number 'twenty-three'. The woman stepped forward, signed for the drugs and as she moved off, passing him, she looked up and ahead; two large blue eyes. Then she was gone, and he had to wait for his Fosinopril. By the time he had collected it and made it to the cashier, she had left the pharmacy. He hurried out searching the broadway up ahead. The crowd of shoppers had grown, and she was nowhere in sight.

*

She had been his first love, now rarely and distantly remembered: half a century ago she was the blue-eyed English blonde of his teenage crush, perfect body, flawless skin, and all of sixteen; every time he saw her sitting there at the reception desk to the Director's suite he held his breath. Too overawed to stop and speak he would find excuses to walk past her many times in a day, until he finally managed a timid 'hello', and she would produce the smile that had undoubtedly won her the job. Then she began showing signs of interest towards him – nothing extravagant or flirty, just little smirks and the occasional in-confidence comment, such as 'Have you seen Mr Conabere's tie today? Dreadful…', a conspiratorial moment shared. She sometimes swept down the wide corridor past the section where he worked, and he came to know the clack of her heels on the polished floor without being able to see through the frosted glass of the partitioned office. And then, eventually, she found reasons to enter the poky little department office where he worked; she would perch like some celestial bird on the corner of his cluttered desk in her form-fitting green uniform, and chat to him. Sing to him, really, because every sound she made was to him a lyric. The two other clerks in the office gaped and flirted with her, but she was his, and they knew it.

*

Within a couple of minutes after leaving the pharmacy, he spotted her up ahead peering in a shop window. Keeping his distance, he followed at her languid pace along the broad walkway, where she kept pausing at shops; she was in no hurry. She wandered into a *Cotton On* store, and began fingering the garments, browsing, no obvious interest in buying anything. Now she was out of sight. He sat down on a seat in the middle of the walkway, opposite the entrance to the store, so he could see when she emerged. Maybe he should just walk up to her and come right out with a declaration of who he was and what his interest in her was. And what was that interest precisely? He was not sure. The desire to know was certainly strong; is she the same person? Does she remember him? What has happened with her all these years? Are these the things he really wants to know, or is it something more, something altogether more selfish, something (he dare not think it) – *conciliatory*? But he doubted he had the courage to approach her. His thoughts were giving him pause: that tumult of desire, so overwhelming in youth, gradually fades and lies buried beneath the canopy of career, marriage, children, travel and all the rest of it, and replaces courage with caution; he was surely too old for impulses.

Over the years there had been one or two moments when she had briefly come back into his mind. Since he retired he had spent much time on the Internet searching for old friends, occasionally from as far back as childhood. It had become absurd, this hunt for aspects of his own past, mindlessly supposing the Net to be a bottomless source of memories, not just the usual social or historical memories, but fatuously, his own personal memories. At times he would idly search for pictures of his parents or grandparents, or some friend he'd not heard from for years. Once he Googled 'Margaret Cole' knowing she would be hardly likely to be found under her maiden name. But with no idea who she might have married, he had no other name to try. And of course no mention of her had ever come up on the screen.

Now she came into view through the wide open doorway of the store, having chosen something from one of the tables, and was taking it to the counter to pay. He waited till she left the store, and then followed her again, keeping about fifty metres behind. The Mall seemed to have become even busier now, the numbers of people to have increased, and several groups of blue-uniformed teenagers were laughing and shouting along the walkway. If only she would stop at one of the coffee stations, sit down and order something, which would give him the opportunity to do likewise at a nearby table, he might start up a conversation in a not-too-forced way. But she showed no sign of doing that. He would somehow have to make a less casual, a more targeted approach.

*

Theirs had been an awakening of bewildered passion, barely out of childhood. This passion had been shaped by movies and pop songs sung by Buddy and Elvis and Patti and Frankie and Ricky and Debbie and all the gang. Their language was only what they had seen and heard on the screen. She would say to him things like 'I love you more than you'll ever know', and even as she spoke they both knew how ridiculous it sounded. But it was all they could do, apart from the innocent, head-spinning kisses. And this language had somehow to dignify the pathetically banal activities they did together – catching the tram to and from work, languishing in the street during lunchtimes, chatting in the office surrounded by others. One exceptional Saturday she had turned up on her bicycle to watch him play cricket, and as he joined his team mates to file onto the field he revelled in their envious looks, and of the opposition players as they eyed her from their seats. She sat on her bicycle steadying herself with one foot on the ground, wearing a cornflower blue dress with a white collar and flared skirt, her blonde ponytail bobbing as she laughed, and the basket on the bicycle carrying a paperback romance; an English rose who might have come straight from a village in Kent. At Tea he brought her into the clubroom to show her off, and as she nibbled her cake and sipped her tea several of his teammates hovered around like bees to a honeypot, ogling entranced by that delectable mouth uttering Home County vowels. He'd done a lot of bowling that afternoon, and when she announced to everyone that his action was 'graceful' he thought his heart would burst with pride.

*

Now she stopped again, this time to sit on a central bench and look at her mobile phone. She was calling a number just as he passed behind her, and he hoped he might hear her voice before moving out of earshot; but she didn't speak. He stopped before a shop window nearby and continued straining to hear if she was saying anything, though he was beginning to feel uncomfortably like a stalker, and tried to look deeply engaged in the contents of the shop window. To his surprise he found he was staring at a Travel Agency, and the window was full of large posters advertising holidays to exotic places. 'Flights to your land of dreams' it said, 'book now to visit historic Europe', scrawled across a picture of the Roman Colosseum. He cast a quick look to where she was seated, still studying her phone. She seemed settled for the moment.

*

The Company always gave its employees a half-holiday on Melbourne Show Day. Margaret came into the office, and asked if anyone was going, because she'd never been, and since the weather was so fine outside, she rather fancied going but had no-one to accompany her. Without hesitation, he leapt in, 'I'll take you,' he said.

'Will you?' she said, in that particularly English way of inflecting a question. 'Oh, that would be grand. Let's go as soon as we finish for lunch!' And so he had at last got his wish — to take out Margaret Cole, indeed to have her all to himself for the rest of the day. It happened that Show Day was also pay-day, and it meant that

15

he could escort her with his pocket full of cash, and on the bus into the city he was filled with pride and power, convinced he was the envy of Melbourne. And as they flopped into their double seat on the near empty bus, she slipped her hand, cool and pale, into his; he looked down at it, and was touched to bursting by her ragged fingers and badly chewed nails. And for the rest of the journey he was blind to whatever was going on in the world out through the bus window.

They went to just about everything at the Show. They saw sheep dog trials and equestrian events, the judging of cows and dogs, of cakes and bottled fruits, they walked through every hall and along every avenue. He bought her show bags containing tiny replicant samples of tomato sauce bottles and jars of jam, fruit cordial and baked beans and of packets of potato chips – all miniatures specially made for the Show. 'I've never seen such things,' she laughed. They walked and looked until it got to be late afternoon and were tired, so they sat in the grandstand and talked; for the first time, properly talked. She had only recently arrived from Bristol with her parents and small brother. This was why she seemed so apart ; she had no school friends, no neighborhood history to draw upon. Family and work were her only social life. He loved the clear, classy English tones of her voice. Occasionally he would say something that would prompt a little spat of pique from her, and in this he perceived a troubling instability that was somehow connected with those ragged fingernails, and he was uncertain at such times where to take the conversation. And there was a sense, too, that she was holding back from him, unwilling to trust. She seemed to tolerate him more than really like him. None of this mattered, so grateful was he just to be with her.

They watched the sun go down in the western sky, then the stand filled up with people, night closed in, and the arena lights switched on to a magical full blaze. After a march-past by Scotch guards the harness racing began, stirring the crowd to enthusiastic cheering. All too soon it was over and the lights were extinguished one by one, and while the patrons drifted away, and the warm October breeze stirred up the day's strewn litter, he resisted as long as he could the admission that it was time to leave. Finally, it was she who said, 'We'd better go home I guess, or they'll end up locking us in for the night.' They caught the train back to the city, and another out to her home in Reservoir, not far from the station. Tired and happy, hands full of show bags, they wandered slowly to her house, and stopped in the dark near the gate in the back fence. He insisted she take all the bags in with her. 'My brother will love the samples,' she said. She thanked him gracefully for the day, and for his generosity, and drew herself into him and rewarded him with a gentle, earnest, soft kiss full and long on his mouth. Then she disappeared through the back gate.

All the way home his heart sang like an ecstatic magpie. It didn't matter that it was past midnight and he'd missed the last bus along Bell Street, and had to walk the whole way, several miles, in the moonless, windy night. It didn't matter that he was flat broke because he'd spent every penny of his two weeks' wages on her. He'd have spent a year's wages on her if I'd had it in his pocket. He didn't care that his mother would almost certainly tear strips off him when she learned he'd spent his whole pay, including her board money, on a girl – a girl she'd never even heard of, and didn't know he was taking to the Show. All that mattered was that he'd achieved his dream, and he was no longer a boy; he was a man, who could escort, pay for, talk with and kiss the most beautiful girl he'd ever laid eyes on.

*

She put away her phone, rose abruptly from the seat and began walking briskly back in the direction she'd come from. There was new purpose in her stride now, and he had to hurry a little to keep up. He found himself behind a slow old couple doddering along arm in arm, and because of a crowd coming from the other direction, was unable to hurry past for what seemed an eternity of stuttering, frustrated steps. In fact, this new development was going to make it difficult now to stop her and say anything – he might have blown his chance. Several more bodies obscured her from sight as she passed the entrance to K-Mart, so he was unsure whether or not she'd gone in; then the bodies parted and he saw her up ahead again. She was checking her phone, standing beside a shop front. *Corner Cuts* said the rectangular shingle just above her head and to the left, *Unisex Hairdresser*. She was either waiting for someone to emerge from the hairdresser's, or she had arranged to meet someone outside it. This was surely his last chance. He must speak to her now, or let the whole opportunity go.

Not wanting it to look obvious he had been following her, he made for the entrance of a shop two or three doors along to her right, then, strolling as casually as his sense of urgency would let him, he made his way along the shop fronts as if interested in their contents and so would appear to come upon her unexpectedly, all the while trying to think what he would say to her. He got to about ten or twelve metres away when she responded to something, looked up from her phone and smiled in his direction. He just had time to say 'Margaret?' when there was a sudden change. Swiftly, confidently, from somewhere behind Kendrick's left shoulder, which was where her gaze had in fact been directed, a man in jeans and a black hoodie walked past him and kissed her on the cheek. It was a careless, proprietorial kiss, reinforced by a protective arm thrown about her shoulders. But her confusion momentarily remained; she had been forming her reply to Kendrick when the interruption came. Indeed, she now went ahead with it.

'Do I know you?' she said to him.

The man moved closer into her, turned and aimed a non-committal smile back at him. He was tallish and had grey stubble on his head and face and was, like Kendrick, an old man about his own age, maybe a little older. Trying to recover his wits, Kendrick responded.

'I… excuse me, I might be mistaken. Is your name Margaret?' he said.

'Yes, it is,' she answered, and waited. His cue was to say her surname, but he hesitated. And then his courage drained away. A sense of hopelessness overtook him. He didn't know what surname to give. In desperation, he went for her maiden name: 'Cole?'

Before she had a chance to reply, the man jumped in. 'Oh, no, sorry fella, I think you've got the wrong person. We're the Serakowskys. Margaret and Paul Serakowsky', and he held out a faux-friendly hand. 'And you are?' he asked. His manner was an impatient mixture of condescension and protectiveness, like *Who the fuck are you and keep away from her anyway.*

In that instant, Kendrick's opportunity was gone. It was hopeless. What could he say? Just go through the ritual of acquaintance? Even if it *was* her, he could not, in this situation, say what lay in his heart to say to her, take her back to the beginning, to the time the disaster occurred and to where he might, with her help, recover the long lost ground; it had been their moment and their moment alone. No one but themselves could go there, could really understand what was needed, first to revisit it then to fix it. And now the moment had passed.

'Oh, it doesn't matter,' he heard himself say, 'I think you're right. I think I've got the wrong person. I'm sorry to have troubled you…' and, desperate to escape humiliation, he hurried off in the direction of the wide Mall entrance. The sliding doors parted and he stepped into a cold blast, to head across to where he could be diminished and swallowed by the car park and its massive canopy of wind and sky and blue air reigning over the field of shining cars loyally awaiting their owners' return. His mind was in a tumult, couldn't recall where he'd left the car, kept thinking how he'd made a complete hash of it, and that he would never now obtain what he now understood he so badly needed – *forgiveness*. He stood in the car park with his hand clutching the side of his balding head, staring at the row of blunt, indifferent vehicle rear-ends in front of him.

*

His first mistake had been to put her on the spot. He'd seen her talking to a tall young man at the reception desk and something in the pit of his gut dropped as he watched her push back coyly in her chair in response to something he said. He was maybe a year or two older than them, someone he'd seen in another part of the building. He'd wanted to fly up there and break in, put a stop to it, but of course he didn't. You can't do things like that. But he worried about it for the rest of the afternoon, waiting for a chance to go and talk to her. Finally, the confrontation came.

'Who was that you were talking to earlier?'

'Chris Beale from the Tack Factory.'

'So, what's he doing over here?'

Her mouth tightened, her eyes avoided him, focused on her typewriter. He was making her angry, but he couldn't help himself.

'He comes over here sometimes to get documents signed,' she said with mock weariness.

'So what was he talking to you about?'

'None of your damn business!' she hissed, this time looking him square in the face with those huge blue eyes, now full of withering fire. He slunk away, crushed.

But he was not finished yet. At five o'clock, leaving the building, he caught her up at the tram stop so that he could ride home with her as usual. At first she was cool, but when he didn't say anything more about Chris Beale, things settled down between them; that is, in so far as what was passing between them could be described as settled. There was something that had stayed uncomfortably private and undeclared about their relationship. It was odd that she had never introduced him to her parents or her brother, though he did catch a glimpse of her father once holding a hose in the front garden, a stocky, pleasant looking man with very English features—clear skin, greying fair hair. But then again, he had never invited her to his house either, so there was the sense in both that they had been playing at romance, and were reluctant to declare it to the world, as if ashamed of it. Truth was, their emotions were uncertain, directionless. Together on the slatted wood seat in the breezy centre section of the tram they once again spoke only the cliches they knew. 'Do you love me?' he asked, pressing into her shoulder. 'I'll always love you,' she crooned, gazing through the window into the distance. But he deplored what they were saying, wincing inside at their crudeness and insincerity. He asked if she would go to the pictures with him the following night, Saturday, and automatically, diffidently, she said 'Okay'. Then she began chewing at her ragged nails.

The second, disastrous, mistake followed. In the foyer the following night he was delighted to find her waiting, bright and cheerful, and looking ravishing in a sleeveless floral summer frock with a low-cut neckline. It had been a hot day, and he told her about his afternoon on the cricket field under a ferocious sun. 'Well I,' she said coyly, 'have been to the beach all day, and gotten myself sunburned. Look.' Her arms and shoulders had a bronze burnish, and heavy make-up amateurishly hid traces of redness on her cheeks or nose. Then, as they took their seats in the cinema, she lowered her voice and laughed, 'Do you want to know something? My back is so sunburned that I'm not wearing any bra. So, there.'

'You're a wicked girl,' he joshed back.

'I am, aren't I?' she giggled.

But he couldn't get the thought out of his head. Whatever the film they were watching, he was not taking it in. Time and again his mind went to her declaration, and what it could mean. Just the fact of her breasts, naked right there under her frock, played on his mind until he could think of nothing else. 'Why did she tell me that? What does she expect me to do? Is she extending an invitation? Is she trying to tease me? That was certainly the tone in her voice'. All through the film he wrestled with desire and fear, until his trembling heart knew that something would happen but not when or how, just that it would happen. And then it did. In the dark he had had his left arm comfortably around her back and resting lightly on her shoulder. Almost involuntarily his hand moved down inside the low-cut bib of her frock and cupped, as one might palm an apple, her naked breast with its hard nipple lodged between his first and second fingers. For a moment she froze, but drew-in a small breath of surprise. Then tersely she whispered, 'No. Take it away.' And he was humiliated, crushed. For the rest of the film they sat together an ocean apart, like strangers. The walk home was an agony of cold silence. He apologized, but she seemed not to be listening. At the gate there was no kiss, no embrace, no words of affection. 'Good night,' she said, and hurried in, slamming the gate behind her. All the long way home he was torn between elation and regret, still reliving the moment of joy, the sheer electric current from her flesh that shot up his arm, and then the withering rebuke. He was certain then that he had done a shameful thing, and that the consequences would be disastrous.

As indeed they were. Plead as he might in the following weeks, she refused to have anything to do with him. She avoided going home with him on the tram, and then, the final ignominy came when he saw her emerging from the building after work and get into a car driven by Chris Beale. The next day, when he asked her to walk with him at lunchtime, unrealistically hoping that he might recover the situation, she said, with a new brutality he could hardly believe, that she was now 'going steady' with Chris Beale, and that she never wanted to talk to him again. Not only was he shattered by this, but he realised he would have to go on seeing her at her desk when he walked past, catching glimpses of her in all parts of the building or going home on the tram, while all the time aching to win her back, knowing he had ruined everything by his own reckless act. He hadn't known how he would bear it; he thought he would die from shame and self-hatred. He thought he should probably kill himself. If only he could go back in time, and undo his terrible mistake. If only she would forgive him.

Wedding Night

In their hotel room Justin moved to the window, shifting the lace curtain aside with the back of his hand and looking out and down Spring Street towards Melbourne's Treasury Gardens. The gold light of the evening sun was tinting the elms and English oaks, casting their long shadows on the grass and deep in behind the lower boughs and shrubbery. Two storeys directly below a line of horse-and-buggies waited in front of the hotel. Across to Justin's left was the imposing colonnade of Parliament House, the scene of momentous decisions, setting the country to war, housing critical debates on the futures of sons and daughters, husbands and wives. Here ego and duty fought bitter campaigns for supremacy.

He was looking to see what the group of anti-conscription protesters were doing; he and Ivy had passed about twenty or thirty of them, chanting and holding placards, assembled on the steps of the building and being marshalled by two policemen as the cab drove up to the hotel. To his left now he could just see the corner of the building from the window, but not the protesters. Feelings had been running high in recent months about the government's proposal to introduce conscription. 'Stupid bastards,' Justin muttered to himself as he left the window. One might have thought their protest had been specifically intended to spoil his wedding day, or to personally insult him as he passed them in his uniform, so intense was his resentment. But he had to take a grip on himself. All that palaver didn't concern him any longer. His decision was made, it was the right one, and despite political quibbles and Ivy's misgivings, he was committed to leaving in the morning with his battalion. He was determined to play his part in this war.

A single night in the Grand hotel hardly counts as a honeymoon, but it was all they had. Even then it would fail. No-one would guess the reason – not the congregation in the church, not the wedding guests at the reception, where Justin put on a brave face all afternoon but ate nothing, not their parents. People were so busy having a good time they simply didn't notice. Ivy knew he was feeling unwell, had been in a fever for the last two days, had struggled to stay on his feet during the ceremony, and when the minister said he could kiss the bride, he'd lurched forward and steadied himself on her shoulder to stop from toppling over onto the floor of the church. Though he had kept it to himself, Justin believed he knew the cause: he was having a reaction to the smallpox vaccination of two days ago, administered by the army doctor. Or it could have been the typhoid shot; but more than likely the multiple smallpox punctures.

Feeling unsteady again, he sat on the edge of the bed. It had been a long, hot day, he was tired and his head ached. He began massaging his temples just as Ivy emerged from the dressing room holding a glass of water and an opened envelope of analgesic powder. She had changed out of her pale wedding jacket and skirt into a full-length deep green evening gown, draped from a high waist such that she looked taller and slimmer than she in fact was. For a disturbing moment, out of nowhere, the thought of decline and disintegration flashed through his mind, a sense that happiness of such intensity cannot last. The thought was only fleeting, for here, in the hotel suite, with her at her loveliest, fashionably dressed, fragrant, all a bonus to the practical intelligence that he always liked about her, he could assure himself that their life together could be a long and happy one. And yet he had chosen to venture into the dark, to put himself in danger. He couldn't, in his youth and inexperience, know the specifics of battle, but he had enough common sense to know it would be horribly uncomfortable at least, and no doubt worse than that. He knew he could die. But he must not dwell on such things, he said to himself. What mattered was that here, with him now, was his wife. Alright, she was unhappy about his going, but she accepted it and his reasons for doing it. That made him proud, proud of her, proud of himself.

'Here, swallow this down. It will help,' she said, and he took the powder from her, tipped it into his mouth and washed it down with the water. She watched him drink the whole glassful in one draught, concern on her face. 'Are you going to be able to eat any dinner?' she said, putting herself next to him on the bed, and laying a hand on his arm. The thought struck him that it was in fact their first moment of physical intimacy as man and wife, and for a moment it made his head swim. They had, of course, touched many times and kissed during their courtship, but now it was different. Now they were a new entity: newlyweds. A sense of expectancy coloured every move, every word they said to each other, because it was all leading to that one necessary act that lay in waiting in the next few hours, as intimidating as any unknown assailant. They both felt this as she let her hand rest a moment longer on the khaki sleeve of his jacket, removing it only when he stood to his feet. He was sweating and looked hot; from his frown he was struggling to stay focussed. She felt helpless to do anything constructive.

'I'd better try,' he said, 'God knows what I'll be getting to eat tomorrow. And I won't have much time for breakfast; I have to be there by nine o'clock.'

Again he went to the window, one arm on the frame for support, while she sat on the pale green quilt, watching him in silence, waiting for him to move. She brushed her hand across the brocaded surface; this was where they would lie together tonight, here they would keep their promise. She would see his naked body, they would touch each other as they never had before, and modesty, self-protection, would go. She wished for it, and wished absolutely that she would be what he needed.

Breaking away from this, leaving the bed, she went over and picked up his peaked cap from the armchair where he'd thrown it when they arrived. Her turning, facing him, prompted him to leave the window and face her too ; she reached up – he was over six feet tall, and she was little more than five feet – and placed it squarely and proudly on his head, its muted Rising Sun badge reflecting a dull light from the electric chandelier, the leather edging on the peak crisp and unstained. He was handsome in his jacket and puttees, with his strong jaw and long-lashed blue eyes, despite his large nose swerving noticeably to one side, and a slightly chipped front tooth.

'I'm pleased you chose to wear your uniform instead of a morning suit. I'm sure everyone was very proud of you,' she said. His arm went round her waist, and she put her face up and shut her eyes; he obliged, softly pressing his mouth against her slightly parted lips, enjoying the dark, sweet hint of alcohol on her breath.

'Not really any choice,' he said, moving back and adjusting the cap so that it sat a little more rakishly on his image in the large wall mirror. 'Remember, I didn't bring any civvies down with me.' And then, with mock formality, and offering his crooked arm, he suddenly said, 'Shall we go down to the dining room, Mrs Debenham?'

But she had to stop and snatch up her white silk wrap, throw it round her shoulders, and then hurry back to his side, slip her arm through his, and a little theatrically, such was their light-hearted mood, they exited their suite to search out the dining room.

This was the one unqualified moment of married bliss they were destined to enjoy on this single night together, thanks to the Australian Army. The initial plan had assumed his leaving for France in February 1917, so the wedding was to be December 9th in Geelong. Both families had sent out the invitations and made the arrangements in plenty of time. Justin had booked a two-week honeymoon at an Otways mountain resort, which would get them back to 'Yawong' in time for Christmas. But they hadn't taken the unpredictability of the Army shipping schedules into account. In September he received a letter saying his battalion's embarkation was being brought forward to October 20th. What with the banns to be read and everyone's arrangements to be changed the soonest they could marry now was October 19th., the day before Justin was to leave. Learning this, the families wanted to put the wedding off altogether. 'Marry in haste, repent at leisure,' Ivy's mother had unhelpfully said, to which she flared, 'It isn't marrying in haste, so it doesn't apply to us. We've been engaged for months!'

The hotel dining room was in turmoil. A waiter had just spilled a tray of plates onto the floor just outside the door to the kitchen, and the pieces had scattered across the room. After a few seconds of silence the room buzzed again with talk punctuated by the clinking of metal on glass; a kitchen hand brought out a broom to sweep up the mess. Light from the dazzling chandeliers refracted and glittered off jewellery, the dressed-up diners weighty in more than one sense and fussed over by penguinesque waiters. Justin and Ivy were unprepared for such a gauntlet as they were led to their table by a flustered looking waitress. Yet, there was a worse trial to face: Justin had forgotten to remove his cap on entering the dining room, forgotten to give it to the waitress to place on a hat stand, so he'd worn it the whole time he passed the tables of chattering diners. This had the effect of making his military uniform – the only one in the room on that evening – even more noticeable, and he squirmed under the looks and nods as he went by, eventually realized what he had done, and blushing snatched it from his head immediately they reached their table. Seated, they waited for a time, reading over their menus, until the drinks waiter returned with a bottle of expensive champagne and, surprisingly, a decorative frame on a stand, which he placed in the centre of their table. It was about eighteen inches high, forming a little arch over the drum-shaped stand on which were poised a miniature bride and groom. The arch over them was entwined with tiny silver and white roses and encrusted with rhinestones. 'A custom of the hotel,' said the waiter as he prepared to pour the champagne into their glasses, 'a gift for our honeymoon diners.'

It was a silly idea in Ivy's view, but she was nevertheless pleased that they'd been singled out, made to feel a little special among this throng of Melbourne notables. Justin was feeling so unwell he hardly noticed it, or the glass of fizzing champagne by his right hand. Nothing on the menu appealed to him. Maybe he would try the oyster soup. They ordered the soup and what the menu described as a 'chicken cutlet' each, and Ivy sipped at her champagne – the first time she'd had it. Suddenly, two tables away, a portly man in a dinner suit stood to his feet, and extending a glass of champagne in their direction, began to talk loudly over the general hubbub. It took Ivy some seconds to realize that the subject of his talk was herself and Justin.

'… drink the health of this fine young patriot and his bride, on what looks very like their wedding day.'

'Hear, hear,' came a man's pompous voice from another table, followed by a general murmur and movement as people turned their attention in the couple's direction. Some of them broke into applause, and then everyone joined in the toast. The pair looked wide-eyed at each other, half wishing the ground would open up and swallow them. A young waiter hurried to top up their champagne glasses, which, guessing the protocol, they raised back at the crowd, and beamed in acknowledgement.

'To the bride and groom,' the portly man called out.

'… bride and groom,' came the straggled general response, and everyone took a sip from their glass. Then the voice boomed out again.

'Young man, we wish you good luck, and thank you and other officers like you for the sacrifice you are making on behalf of the

Empire and all of us who treasure it.' Again he raised his glass, this time above his head, and called out, 'Ladies and gentlemen, the King.'

'The King!' came the vigorous response around the room. And everyone took another sip, before with noisy commotion resuming their seats.

By this time Justin was flushing and hot, with sweat beading on his face and running freely down his ribs under his shirt. He didn't want the champagne, which he was sure would only make him worse. But he did drink down two full glasses of water from the jug on the table, his hand shaking so badly that the jug rattled against the glass. Obviously, his fever was not getting any better. Ivy reached over and touched his hand, as if to steady it.

'Stupid bugger,' said Justin, 'I don't need his fatuous speeches.' Ivy pulled a scrunched face.

'Still, it was nice of him – nice of them – to notice,' she said.

'Well, he isn't that sharp,' he muttered, 'he didn't even notice I'm not an officer.'

Ivy recalled that his choice had puzzled and dismayed his father and sisters. Surely, they said, with his private school education and the family's social position, he was entitled to a commission?

'I don't know, and I don't care,' Justin told them, 'I'm enlisting as a private and that's the end of it. I'm not doing it to give orders, or big note myself. I just want to do my bit, in the same way that others are. If I'm going to be promoted I want to earn it in the ranks, not because I'm an Old Geelong Grammarian.'

As his father had said on the day his letter of enlistment came through, he very likely would not have qualified for a commission anyway, with no military experience to offer. Nor was Ivy bothered about it – what did she care what rank he was? And in any case, she had read somewhere that the officers were at greater risk than the ordinary men, because the enemy in the field was always looking to target them first, so she was happy for him to stay a private.

She finished her soup and roll; she was hungry, she realized, having eaten little all day, and been too busy at the reception to do more than snatch a single sandwich. Justin put down his spoon and wasn't finishing his. She sensed that there was more to his agitation than his fever. There was a tense irritability in his manner, and she had a premonition that he was about to target her.

'Maybe you'll be able to manage the chicken,' she said. But when it came he did little more than play around with it, forked a few peas into his mouth, drank more water, and finally pushed it away. Meanwhile, she wolfed hers down, and was wondering about the dessert.

'There certainly isn't anything wrong with *your* appetite,' he said. It was almost an accusation.

'I'm famished,' she said, and went quiet.

'That rabble outside Parliament House,' Justin said, 'how many would you say there were?' So he was still bothered about that.

'I don't know – twenty or so perhaps.'

'Bloody traitors, the lot of them. Don't you agree?'

Since she felt his anger was being partially directed at her, she instinctively moved into resistance.

'Isn't that putting it too strongly?'

'Too strong? Rubbish.'

'I wouldn't agree with forcing men to fight, either.'

'What?'

'If they don't want to go, they shouldn't have to.'

'Are you defending gutless bastards?'

'I don't know if they're doing it because their cowards or not, but as my father says, what use is it to send men who are either too cowardly or too unsympathetic to the cause? They wouldn't be good soldiers either way, and might let their mates down.'

'It's their duty, that's the long and short of it.'

'It might be more a question of duty if their families were under threat. But many people don't agree with this war. Yes, you see the virtue of it, but many don't, and they should be free to choose, surely? No, I think the fighting should be done by volunteers, not conscripts.'

'Freedom has its limits. We're part of an Empire, like a team, and we enjoy many of the benefits of that; we can't just pick and choose which activity to support. You're either a member of the team or you're not. It's a question of honour.' He drank more water and pushed his chair back from the table, slapping his napkin down angrily so that it fell on his plate of food.

Ivy hated the turn the conversation had taken; this was not what she wanted, not what they should be doing. Justin was now in a bad state, she could see. She took herself under control, silently admonished herself for her thoughtlessness, reached across the table and this time took his hand in hers.

'I'm sorry,' she said, 'Let's not have this quarrel, not on this night. Let's end this stupid discussion and just try to be happy in the time we have left. Try and eat something.'

He met her words by pulling a wry smile, and returned the pressure of her hand. He watched her finish her champagne. His stood untouched. He looked around and noticed several people at the other tables watching them with concerned faces, obviously aware of what had been taking place.

'I suppose it's just the thought of those buggers out there, throwing muck at men who are prepared to give their lives for this country. Your father's right about one thing – I wouldn't want the likes of them beside me when the chips were down,' he said.

'Let's go back to the room?' she said, 'We could get them to send up some tea or coffee,'

'Tea might help,' he says, 'because the aspirin doesn't seem to be doing much good.'

And so they ran the gauntlet again, and the nods of approval were even more pronounced. Ivy wondered whether these were purely conventional wedding sentiments, or a statement of political solidarity, given the presence of the anti-conscripters outside. She had no doubt that all of these nodders would be eagerly voting 'yes' in the coming referendum.

They did not see each other undress. The Grand Hotel boasted private bathroom facilities and a dressing room in its best suites, which allowed couples to prepare for bed separately. So when she entered the bedroom in her full-length, neck-to-ankle white nightdress, he was already there in his similarly long, but pale blue, nightshirt. He dimmed the lights and slid back the curtain from the window, which he'd opened to admit a cooling breeze, and the faint light from a first-quarter moon. Now he stood beside the window looking thoroughly unhappy, whether from apprehension or illness, or both, she couldn't tell.

So pleased was she with the nightdress she'd found in Buckley and Nunn's that she bought herself two the same: fine white Cambric with delicate embroidery around the collar and cuffs. And two, she told herself, might well be necessary should she bleed, which was quite likely - her mother's idea, one of several sensible pieces of advice she had given Ivy. For all her disdain for fuss over the everyday, her mother was good on organisational matters, and had done an excellent job on the wedding and reception. Ivy had inherited a similar, almost a designer's, mind for order. She was conscious of the drawbacks in this, the potential to kill spontaneity and romance. A secret cause, waged since puberty, since she began taking an interest in males as such, and in the tactics of adult relationships, was to maintain a balance between heart and head. She was not going to be one of those girls who gush over handsome men and think life is all moonlight cruises and looking pretty, but neither did she want the bluestocking way, or to try to live to some sort of methodical program. Balance was the important thing, she told herself. Often.

Silence descended on them both, standing on opposite sides of the bed, neither prepared to make the next move of pulling back the bedclothes and getting in. Cumulatively, the beige-toned luxury of the room, its sumptuous formal drapes, its magnificent Persian rugs, the floral arrangements in *art nouveau* vases, the huge baroque gold framed mirror, the Queen Anne furniture, like the space of the room itself, dwarfing them, conspired to cow them into submission. Language had abandoned them, and in their heads whirled a chaos of disconnected words and phrases, unutterable. The longer the silence went on the more the tension was going to mount between them. This is absurd, thought Ivy, and promptly, bravely, she walked around from her side of the bed to Justin's. She threw her arms around him, so that she was front-on to his left side, pressing against his bicep and hip. The contours of flesh under their light nightclothes, and the shock it produced, were a pleasant surprise.

'This is not going to be easy for either of us, is it?' she said.

He placed his arms about her waist; the body beneath her nightdress was different from the feel of her when covered in clothing and heavy undergarments. An impulse in his groin made him instinctively back his lower body away from hers. She felt it too, but she counteracted his movement, pushing herself in closer, urging their lower bodies into frank pressure with each other, and as she did this she reached up and kissed him, hungrily working her lips on his. But when they parted and looked directly at each other's face, he was frowning, and his eyes conveyed a confusion of fever, shame, even terror. Nothing was happening in his groin. Those brief stirrings had now completely gone.

'Let's get into bed,' she said, and wrenched back the covers, sat herself down on the bed edge and, because she was now lower than his standing form (level with his penis, it occurred to her), she looked down, noticing that he still had his black socks and garters on.

'Look at you,' she mocked, 'take them off for goodness sake!' He laughed with her, and steadying himself against the bedhead, slid them off one at a time.

She then rolled backwards and lay crosswise against the white sheets, her legs dangling over the side, too short to reach the thick rug. He fell forward beside her, kneeled upright, then, taking up her covered legs, dragged her around so she was now straight on the bed, with him positioned above and beside her. This was the moment when he could, and should, have pushed back the nightdress, gently parting her legs and edged himself between. But he hesitated; anticipations of tomorrow morning's tasks – getting to the barracks, then to the wharf, flashed through his mind. He tried to force himself back to Ivy, this sweet body, this face anxiously awaiting his next move. The room around him seemed askew, his hands difficult to control as if they were separate beings, his breathing short and his heart acting like some bird trying to get out. But not from desire, not from anticipation; it was fever, overmastering him. Was it fever, overmastering him? He didn't really *want* to do it. He didn't really have the desire he was supposed to have. He would be happy to just kiss her again and leave it at that. Why would that not be enough? In desperation, he tried to make it happen, and did push back the nightdress, parted her legs, confronted the dark bush, moved himself between her legs, lowered himself to kiss her and push in at the same time. But it was no use. He was ridiculous, and defeated. He was shamed. Falling away and to the side, he rolled on his back and whispered, 'Bugger me; I can't. I can't.' Tears of frustration welled up and slid down his temples. He put his hands to his face in embarrassment.

Pushing her face into his neck, Ivy predictably said, 'It doesn't matter, it isn't your fault; it's those awful vaccinations. There isn't anything the matter with *you*, you're normal, healthy, and I know you love me and would be able to show me that you do if it weren't for your fever. Please, please, don't concern yourself over it. Maybe we can try again later – when we've had a little sleep. I'll wake you.'

But he hardly heard her words. Some other voice was saying things to him, saying, 'And was it that? Was it the fever only?' Wasn't there something else, something taking away the need, something deadening his feelings, something that actually was insisting that, when it came down to it, he had no actual interest in her? The thought horrified him, and he tried to dismiss it.

They lay there, wrapped into each other, listening to the noises from Spring Street, the trotting of horse-and-carriage, the screech of cable trams turning into Bourke street, the chug of the odd motor car, the occasional cries from vendors; eventually all went quiet, leaving only the distant sound of gurgling water from the Stanford Fountain across the road, the generous bequest of a contrite felon who had atoned for his crimes in the best way he knew how.

A couple of hours into the night Ivy woke and looked across at her sleeping husband. His nightshirt was quite damp with sweat. She placed a hand on his forehead, but it was not hot – his fever had broken, and he was deeply asleep. She couldn't bring herself to wake him. She lay there, thinking. There will be plenty of other times in the future, when we'll be able to make love. The War will be over, he will come home and everything will be normal. What would our future be? Living on the farm with his parents and sisters. The thought of it was comforting. Even before they had any children, there would be a sense of family. She was lucky in that. She would be able to get on with her drawing and painting, and the girls would look after the house. She didn't feel the need to get involved in the farm itself, but she would be a farmer's wife, something she'd never imagined when she was a girl. But it might just suit. It might just be the life she needs. As she lay back down she slipped here hand beneath the pillow, and felt a soft material there; oh yes, she remembered, the other nightdress, neatly folded and ready, just in case. Won't need it now. Mustn't forget it when I pack tomorrow.

When she woke in the morning Justin was already up and dressed, and busying himself with his kitbag. The drapes had been pulled back, and sunlight streamed in through the full-length windows, so harshly bright it was almost like an assault. She winced and squealed and shoved her face into the pillow for protection. He laughed at her.

'Come on wife, up you get; I've got half an hour to get some breakfast and get down to Albert Park!' She sat up, yawned and stared back. He looked so young and handsome in his uniform, so full of energy, and strong, as if nothing in the world could have the impudence to harm him. He would be all right, she told herself, they would be all right, even the world would be all right, once people finally came to their senses. And at that she leapt out of bed and felt the soft warmth of the rug on her bare feet.

The Rodin of Syndal West

This is not an especially kind story. But then my stepfather was not an especially kind man. He was never abusive or violent, but he did keep all expressions of feeling tightly closed down, especially the more benevolent ones. Part of it was vanity over his chronic dermatitis, which made his hands and face red raw and the skin flaky – a legacy of his war service in New Guinea – and much of it was an intense and debilitating shyness: whenever visitors came, as they often did on a Sunday, when my mother would go to great lengths to tidy the house, put flowers around, bake scones or a cake, and put on her best dress and freshest face, Harold would stay in the bathroom the whole afternoon – and I mean the whole afternoon, two-till-five ! My mother would be chatting away with the guests – often it was Harold's own mother and brother – embarrassed and calling to him to come out and socialize, but generally he wouldn't emerge from his endless ablutions, or whatever he did in there, until the very moment the guests were actually taking their leave, putting on their coats and approaching the open front door.

'Ah', he would call after them as they shuffled down the front path towards their car, 'wouldn't you like another drink or something ?' This, after the plates and cups had been cleared away and the leftovers back in the cupboard half an hour ago!

Embarrassment, shyness, but also a kind of arrogance. There was the pretence of having to look his best for the occasion, and the implicit plea for sympathy for his social unease. There was also an antisocial sense that he didn't really care to engage with people, that it was all too trivial, and that he had nothing much to say in this particular setting. If you saw him with his mates in the pub, of course, he was talking and laughing his head off. That is another story. But domestically, he wasn't interested.

And yet it was precisely this failure to communicate that led to his adoption of an unlikely hobby. All the years I was at home under his quasi-paternal reign he never showed the slightest interest in handiwork about the house. I always assumed he didn't know how to do any of it; he didn't own a hammer or a saw, or a screwdriver, let alone anything as sophisticated as a power drill. His tools of trade – he was a butcher – were left conveniently at work, so he couldn't even resort to his meat cleaver to cut off an end of wood, or his carving knife to tighten a screw; my mother did all that, usually with a bread and butter knife or the heel of a shoe for a hammer, unless she was inspired enough to find a way of using the immovably rusty old shifter that had lain in the kitchen drawer for years going back to when her first husband, my father, was alive. She would bash at the screw with the shifter until it submitted and lay embedded and mangled in its wooden seating. The house, as a consequence, was afflicted with doors (cupboard and entry) that wouldn't open and shut properly, towel rails that sloped at crazy angles, gate hinges and latches that wobbled and dangled, and handles everywhere that came off in your hand. In all of this there was, certainly, an element of justifiable self-indulgence, since the house did not belong to us but to the Housing Commission of Victoria, who were supposed to be responsible for all maintenance, but were notoriously slack, or to be fair, could only be expected to come if they were actually notified of the problem, which they rarely were. Harold was one of those who believed that any energy spent on repairs, improvement, redecoration or just plain functionality was totally wasted, because the main aim in life should be to get *out* of our dependence on the damn Housing Commission, not hunker down and accommodate oneself to it. So, the more derelict the house became, the more motivated one was to ignore it and ultimately escape.

This view was, I know, anathema to my mother. Especially when it came to the garden. But of course in the mid 1950s, when she worked full-time, looked after three demanding children (four if you count my stepfather) and cooked, cleaned and washed with no help from anyone, she simply didn't have the time for anything else, not even gardening. That particular joy, along with many others she was looking forward to when they finally did buy their own house, had for the time being to be deferred.

The consequence was that our garden, as such, didn't exist. We had a back yard of dry grass in the summer and mud in the winter. Perhaps I'll qualify that: grass and iron hard clay with three-inch wide cracks in the summer, and mud coated with soggy onion-weed in winter. Nothing useful would grow in it; we had a slowly dying lemon tree beside our concrete path for ten years, never producing a single lemon, looking like an item in a set for a Samuel Beckett play. My mother, in what time she could muster away from her chores, did plant the odd camellia and photinia, but these struggled through umpteen seasons to achieve a pathetic knee-height. For a time my younger brother Rook and I took turns to cut the front grass – it was hardly lawn – with the Victa mower she optimistically bought one Xmas, and when I left home in my late teens Rook took over that burden as his own specialism. Harold did nothing.

He saw one use and one use only for the back yard – to park his blue 1956 FE Holden Station Wagon in it. Now this seemingly sensible move was in fact one of the more notable pieces of idiocy that marked his time in that house. Ours was a corner block, so it was possible to take a car into the back yard via the side fence, in which a double gate had been provided. But there was no garage. In winter Harold would open the gate and catapult the Holden from the street directly into the deep, intractable bog of a back yard to stand overnight, in the mad hope of driving it straight out early in the morning to go to work. Of course, he mostly ended up down to the axles in black ooze. We would watch him from the kitchen window trying to lay something under the wheels for grip – bits of board he had picked up somewhere for the purpose, a sheet of corrugated iron, the rubbish bin lid, old shoes or a cushion he found in the woodshed, my best cricket pads would you believe – anything his desperate and disorganized mind could come up with that might get him out of the bog, but rarely did. The solution that too often prevailed was that we – including my small sister Lizzie and our boarder Pattie – got out in our various states of undress and pushed the car, engine roaring and wheels spinning, out of the mire, and all afterwards stumping back into the house in nighties and pyjamas spotted with gunk. And this of course was only the mornings when the Holden, forever out in the elements, would actually start; since Harold had no idea what mysteries took place under the bonnet of a car, because he never looked there, its points, its plugs and leads, its battery were all in near-useless condition, and worked more by luck than design. On those mornings it stubbornly refused to start he usually gave up and, stony faced, went back to bed, leaving the car sitting in the mud in the yard.

Such was the tenor of life under Harold's reign during my mid-teen years. It would have been a depressing time except that we all for different reasons looked upon it as temporary. My mother had a clear goal – to save enough money to build a decent home of her own; she'd been planning it for years. Harold's contribution would basically be to qualify for a war-service loan. I was looking to make an early exit from the nest, which I did the week after I completed my National Service training; I'd made a close friend at Puckapunyal, and we got ourselves a flat in St. Kilda road and took on the World Out There together. Rook was spending increasing time at the homes of a wide circle of mates, though he was to remain nominally living at home for a few years yet. It was he who told me the details of the events I'm about to relay, because I had during this time all but lost touch with my family.

My mother's dream was realised in a brand-new brick veneer at Syndal West – a long way out certainly, but to her great pride it was in the *eastern suburbs*, a virtual Camelot in her hopes during the worst years immediately after the War. She got a better paid, less time-consuming job, money and time were found to establish a nice new garden, Pattie left to get married, Lizzie started secondary school and helped about the house, my brother lived an increasingly peripatetic (some would say vagrant) life among mates, girlfriends and fast cars, and Harold left butchery to take up – wait for it – part-time taxi-driving; my caution here is to indicate, if it had not already become clear, that a worse driver and less car-savvy Australian male could hardly have been put behind any steering wheel, let alone that of a taxi. But we'll let this likely shambles go undescribed, since none of us really knows how it went apart from Harold himself and his poor anonymous passengers. He did once allow the head of his taxi engine to completely crack in half by failing to put water in the radiator. And he broke an axle one day when he saw a pile of bluestone pitchers on the side of the road, and loaded up not only the boot but also the back seat with them. What it did mean – being part-time – was that Harold found himself with daylight hours on his hands and a newfound motivation to contribute something to the general progress and well-being of the new home.

That something turned out to be concreting.

It was a gift that revealed itself only gradually, and almost by accident; my mother wanted some edging around the garden beds and suggested that Harold buy a bag of ready-made mixture at the hardware store and do it himself. The modest success of this was a nourishment to his confidence, and so he extended the edging right around the garden and along the many metres of front, side and rear fences. It took him months of patient trowelling, but he clearly enjoyed the work, and managed a respectable degree of neatness and consistency. A mate had offered to sell him a second-hand concrete mixer, but the artisan spirit had taken hold of him, and he doggedly stuck to mixing it by shovel on a piece of flat tin. Over the following months he made paths in the front and rear gardens; slurry-rendered the brick incinerator; built and odd shaped concrete pond with pointed lumps in the middle, meant to be miniature mountains but looking more like upturned legs of lamb; made a concrete set of corner shelves beside the back door that somehow incorporated rendered pieces of chipboard and two plastic ice cream containers; a masterpiece of modernist asymmetry, it was, he always maintained, unfinished, but my brother quipped that it was unstarted, since nothing could possibly be held on its badly skewed shelves; made a concrete letterbox that proved too heavy to carry, so it remained abandoned down the corner of the yard for years; lovingly fashioned a barbecue, with an old iron stove door for a cookplate, and two nautical-looking chimneys extending upward from the back. He forgot, however, to provide draught openings for the fire and so it produced much smoke but no heat; my brother still retains a vision of him wincing at stoking a hopelessly suffocated fire while smoke clouds billowed from the two chimneys like a ship at full speed.

Shouting through clouds of smoke, my mother sought the fate of two pieces of rump and four sausages she'd given him to cook, and when they were finally rescued from the smoke the steak was grey and raw and the sausages the same. Nothing would ever cook on that barbecue, and it was abandoned after the first few failed attempts.

Mum got to the stage of advising him to slow down, as his artful enthusiasm was threatening to overwhelm her dreams of a garden of natural beauty. But once started, he proved hard to stop. She was alarmed one day to find him concreting the wrought iron posts of the carport — all the way up, so that it looked like a four-poster bed made of playdough.

But the crowning moment of his career as a sculptor in concrete came the day he decided to solve two problems with the one stroke. For some time my mother had been pleading with Rook to remove his old Ford Anglia from under the carport in the front driveway. He'd been 'working on' the engine for almost two years with the aim of competing in rallies, during which time it hadn't moved from its spot, and was already rusting and flat-tyred. These were days when he would come home maybe once a week to drop in his dirty laundry, and yet again outline his plans to lower the head of the Anglia, fit racing suspension, a Lukey muffler and have it resprayed purple.

'In your dreams', said our newly smart-mouthed sister Lizzie. But on this Saturday morning my mother had had enough. 'No!' she banged the saucepan on the stove, 'I want that wreck off the premises by the end of this weekend, so Harold can put the Holden under the carport'.

'Okay, okay, okay', said Rook, but by lunchtime he had been picked up at the front gate by a very hot blonde in a Triumph TR3, which immediately disappeared with them in the direction of the Dandenong Ranges, and not only was nothing done about the Anglia's removal, but the family didn't clap eyes on Rook again for another fortnight.

Now for some time mum had talked of putting a back patio outside the double doors of the family room, which to that stage just had a step that led out into the back yard. Taking his cue from the finality in my mother's voice, Harold apparently had come to a firm resolution of his own, one that he reckoned would kill two birds with one stone. The next weekend Keith, his one-eyed mate from the RSL, agreed to come over in his Valiant and together they would take matters into their own hands. Conveniently for Harold it coincided with mum spending the day over at her friend Madge's house in Oakleigh, a little pleasure she had kept for herself ever since she married Harold. Mum and Madge liked to go to Bingo together, and reminisce all day about old times. It turned out to be convenient for Harold because now he would be able to carry out his plan for the Anglia uninterrupted and unsupervised; while the cat's away, and so on.

Working as fast as their unfit bodies would allow, Harold and Keith outlined a rectangle about three by two metres in the lawn and, over the course of the day, dug it out to about just over a metre deep, one end finishing almost at the step outside the double doors of the family room. They then took down a section of timber fence behind the carport, allowing a clear access into the back yard, and started the job of pushing the Anglia through into the yard. But they couldn't budge her. It was not just the flat tyres stopping her, but they worked out that Rook must have been working on the gearbox or the differential, and the wheels were not able to rotate. 'I know,' said Harold, 'we'll use the Valiant.' There was just enough width between the side fence and the car port to get Keith's Valiant past the Anglia into the yard, and by hitching a tow rope to the Anglia they towed it, wheels locked and scraping the driveway in protest, into the yard to stand beside the freshly dug pit.

At this point they clearly felt some unwanted openness to public gaze from the street, so they went about replacing the section of fence they had taken down, thus ensuring complete privacy for their bizarre plan. Pushing and pulling, grunting and cursing, the two friends eventually manoeuvred the Anglia into the pit, where it sat sadly but neatly, the lawn butting up to the same level as its window bottoms. Then they worked feverishly to backfill around its wheels, door skirts and bumper bars until it was securely half-buried, with its off-white cabin top sitting above the level of the lawn like some enormous odd-shaped mushroom. The pile of leftover dirt offered them no problem; it was shovelled in through the open windows into the cabin, filling it level with the dashboard and burying the seats, window-winders and steering wheel. By late afternoon they were leaning on their shovels, panting heavily and admiring their handiwork, which they continued on the patio step after Harold cracked open a nice large brown bottle of cold Victoria Bitter.

'Of course, this is only half the job', he pointed out to Keith.

'Why's that?'

'Got to build the patio yet'.

'We won't do that today, surely?'

'No, no. That'll take me a while.'

'Shit!' said Keith over the rim of his beer, and staring fixedly over Harold's shoulder with the look of a man who had just seen his last twenty dollar note eaten by a camel.

'What?'

'The Valiant.'

The blue vehicle stood in silent admonition before their eyes, with the fence intact and imprisoning them all, Harold, Keith, Anglia and the Valiant, *inside* the yard; grave-digging had blinded them to all lesser excitements, and they had forgotten to drive the Valiant out before they replaced the fence. It was evening and totally dark by the time they got the fence down and up again, then Keith drove off home for his tea, and my mother returned, after walking the block from the bus stop. The first thing she noticed as she came up the driveway was the missing Anglia, and the two-tone green Holden smugly occupying its place.

'What've you done with it?' she asked.

'Oh,' said Harold, 'it's in the back yard.'

'The back yard? How?'

'We managed.' Harold's taciturnity again.

She went into the kitchen, turned on the outside light, and looked out the window into the yard. She stared for a good twenty seconds, failing to see the Anglia.

'Where?'

'Outside the double doors.'

Then, in disbelief at what she could see, 'Oh My God. Is that the Anglia?'

'A bit of it.'

She didn't know whether to laugh or cry, and in the end, she did a little of both. 'Nobody has a car buried in their garden!' she wailed.

'It's okay, you won't see it,' he said. 'Not when I'm finished.'

'What are going to do with it?'

'You'll see,' said Harold, 'eventually. But from now on the Holden is in the car port.'

As he said, it was only half the job done. Over the next week Harold's concreting gifts were to be brought fully into play. Many bags of Portland cement were delivered, devotedly mixed, and carefully carried and applied every time Harold could find a chance to work on it. Holding boards were put in place, and shovelful after shovelful was layered on and around the Anglia roof, which gradually disappeared from sight and became the foundation for the new patio. The roof itself had posed a momentary problem, being a tad too high for a comfortable exit from the double doors of the house, but Harold solved this by hacksawing the front and rear roof supports through, smashing the windscreen and rear window, and forcing the roof down to just above the level of the bonnet. From then on it was just a matter of building up a good six or eight-inch layer of concrete over the whole body, carefully filling in the tricky corners with his trowel and spatula, and then with the sides walled straight with boards and the top smoothed out with a nice long piece of board for a level, a perfect rectangular slab was achieved. When it was finished and dry it stood gleaming and pale grey, a patio you could step onto directly from the family room for many a happy outdoor gathering.

'Will it hold the weight of the barbecue?' my mother wondered.

'Don't be silly', said Harold. Nothing could shake his hard-won confidence in concrete.

'What will we tell Rookie about the Anglia?' she asked.

'We've solved his problem for him', said Harold. And indeed, in his heart, my brother always knew that Harold was right in this view, despite his threats to sue Harold for stealing his car.

A dozen years later my mother retired, and they sold the house and moved to Queensland. I believe she hoped that a new beginning would mean an end to Harold's career in concrete sculpture. It didn't. Indeed, the very day they moved he retrieved a standard ashtray from the skip out front, where my mother had thrown it; no one in the house smoked anymore. What did he do with the standard ashtray? He used it as the substructure for a concrete birdbath that he completed within two months of taking up residence in the new house, and placed in the unfenced front garden. By this time he had discovered a new word for his activities; recycling. It was newly heard from everyone's lips as a universal Good Thing, and Harold began thinking of himself not as a mere concreter, or even as an artist, but as an environmentalist. No doubt the new neighbours were in for some surprises as Harold made his mark on the streetscape over the coming years. But none more surprised than the new owners back in Syndal West would be, should they one day have cause to investigate the foundations of their very handsome back patio.

The Visit

The storm had been threatening all morning; he'd watched the build of dark clouds through the carriage window; the thought of leaving his warm seat in the train and heading out into the cold and wet had filled him with dread. Standing on the platform of Tula station staring through the drifting snowflakes at the disappearing tracks, he wondered whether an act of will would make the train go on to Kozlova Zaseka. But the station master had been adamant as the handful of passengers spilled out of the two carriages:

'Eto ne Kozlova, net', he barked from within the upturned lapels of his thick overcoat, his cap pulled down so low you could barely see his eyes, the dirty blond moustache completely obscuring his mouth; his emphasis suggested he knew there were foreigners in the seats, and needed to make himself clear. Making his way along the platform his squat body rocked from side to side, signalling a hip condition; he began busying himself closing the carriage doors, which he did with the noisy authority of a caretaker locking up a building for the night.

Now to find a carriage to get to the estate. How far might it be? It must surely be ten, fifteen miles. He opened part of the inadequate map he'd bought in Moscow, but his knowledge of Russian was so poor he couldn't make sense of the names, though he could guess at them and get a rough sense of the direction and distances. Passing out through the station gate he saw an empty four-wheel cab standing in the roadway, the small black horse stark before the white curtain of falling snow in the trees behind; the heavily rugged-up driver was bent over as though asleep. He approached and called, *'Perevoski?'* He'd learned the word during his week in Moscow.

The man stirred and looked at him without enthusiasm, and little comprehension.

He held up the map. '*Yasnaya Polyana*' he said.

The man shrugged in such a way as to indicate either lack of interest, ignorance of what he'd said, or permission for him to climb into the carriage. Youthful optimism decided him upon the latter, and he threw his knapsack up onto the seat and followed it in under the protective hood of the cab. In fact it gave little protection from the blizzard as he pressed back into the seat. They moved slowly forward, the wheels crunching on the slush of snow and gravel. The driver said nothing the whole time; the only sound came from the soft padding of the horse's hoofs as it clomped through what was now deepening snow, snow building noticeably on the muddy road. All the time he was trying to take in the strangeness, the alienating feel, of the scene about him while at the same time trying to control his mounting excitement. Was he really getting this close to his goal?

After several turns into cross-roads and twists through open farmland with scatterings of village houses visible, and with no sun to take his bearings from, he had lost all sense of direction. His fate was entirely in the driver's hands. They must have been travelling some fifteen minutes in the open countryside, it's green disappearing fast under the increasingly heavy snowfall, when the driver let out an angry cry and stamped his boot on the carriage floor. Then he pulled the horse over to the side and stopped. He said nothing, just sat there staring at the horse's rump, and waiting.

'What the trouble?'

The driver continued to stare ahead. '*Net, plokhoy sneg.*' he said, and gestured widely with one hand at the expanse of white fields around them.

He understood it meant the weather was too bad.

Eventually the man turned round and waved his arm back towards the direction they had come from. '*Net dal'she*', he said several times, '*Net dal'she*', and waved an open palm, indicating 'no'; he wanted to go no further. Perhaps he wanted to go back to the station. No, no, he thought to himself, I've come this far, I can't give up when I'm so close. Surely we can keep going until we see the estate, at least. But how to argue with the man?

'*Net, net*' he said, as assertively as he felt he could without sounding like a bully. '*Yasnaya polyana, da, da,*' and impatiently giving up the scramble for Russian words, he pleaded *we must keep going to the estate – to Yasnaya polyana – we must at least get to the entrance*'.

He reached in his pocket and took out a handful of kopecks. The driver looked down at the coins, and – oh, the incongruity of those dirty, thick peasant fingers and the delicacy with which they were being employed – carefully selected three twenty kopeck pieces, and grunted an acknowledgement. But he was not going to resume the journey.

'*Plokhoy sneg, plokoy sneg,*' he repeated, and began to pull the horse's head around to the left. This was it, he said to himself, I can't retreat, I must go on, and grabbing his knapsack he leapt from the turning carriage into the roadside slush. The driver uttered growls of disapproval; '*Ah, ah, ah*' he was saying, as he clucked encouragement to the horse to move off.

Trotting beside the carriage he pleaded, '*Which way to Yasnaya polyana?*' The response was another expansive wave, indicating a long distance in the general direction they'd been heading and to the right. And that was that. He stood in the middle of the red-brown slush of the road with its white snow edging, watching the rear end of the carriage diminish as it trailed off into the distance.

So he began on foot, trudging through mud pools and then moving over onto snow so dry and powdery that his boots squeaked as they pushed through it, into the cut of a bitter wind that slanted the snow almost horizontally into his face. He could still make out enough of the road to see that it went in the general direction the driver's wave had indicated, and so he followed that. Everywhere was eerily deserted; he was now quite alone and dependent on hopeful guesses as to where he should direct himself.

It took some effort to keep moving, and he was already feeling the shock of the cold. This was not helped by the inadequacy of his clothing – an oilskin coat over a corduroy hiking suit – which gave him little warmth; but the weather had been mild until this storm had hit. Pain affected his nose and ears, which he supposed was better than numbness. That would have been a bad sign. But the cold through his back and shoulders was worrying; clearly he was losing body heat. If he could just keep on the move until he could find shelter, the storm might pass and visibility improve.

After ten minutes or so he could make out up ahead what looked like a farmhouse, resting on the shoulder of a slope. He might get some directions there. Heading off the road he stumped up a rudimentary driveway, but as he got closer it became clear that it was only a large barn, and there was no house in sight. In an adjoining paddock a bay draught-horse stood at the fence looking at him expectantly. A coating of snow lay along its back and haunches.

'Sorry mate, I've nothing for you,' he muttered, and was surprised at the level of resonance of his voice, carrying into the distance. The horse didn't move. He knew horses, had grown up with them in Queensland, and could see this was an old fellow probably feeling the cold. No doubt he would have liked to be in the barn, but was prevented by the fence running between it and the paddock. The barn door was slightly open, so he peered inside. It was largely empty, save for a dray and a few hay bales. He picked up a bale and carried it out to the horse, who snorted approval as he approached. He dropped the bale over the fence, and as the horse bent his neck to pull at the hay he scooped the snow off its back with his cupped hand.

'There you go,' he said, 'that'll keep you happy for a while.'

Then the snow began to get heavier, so he went back to the barn and stood just inside the doorway peering out at the bleaching terrain. Inside it was dry and protected from that excruciating wind, so he dragged up another hay bale and sat on it, placing his knapsack beside him. He could have dropped off to sleep easily, but he had no intention of allowing that to happen. He dug his pocket watch out of his vest pocket; the time was 11.07 am. Must not rest long, must find the estate in the next hour or so, or he could miss the train back to Moscow, which he knew left at 5.20 that afternoon. Of course if he found the estate he might not need to catch it. Perhaps, he fantasised, he would be invited to stay over; perhaps they would become engaged in a discussion in which he would acquit himself well, and be asked to supper and a bed. Could such things possibly happen? After five minutes or so sitting he knew he would have to get moving, or he might be tempted to lie against the hay bale and take a nap, which would be disastrous. No, must get on.

He stood and moved to the barn doorway, looking for the road. Now the snow was easing off, and he could see farther into the distance. Heaving the knapsack back onto his shoulders he trudged out. He must have walked for another fifteen minutes without seeing anything of interest. Then up ahead the road seemed to disappear. There was nothing to indicate which direction he should take. In the distance a thick clump of trees or tall shrubs might at least offer shelter from the bitter wind, so he made for that. It turned out to be the beginning of a dense forest, and while it certainly was calmer once he entered it, its darkness and relative stillness produced a different, penetrating kind of cold. This was a good moment to pause and take stock, take some sustenance, so using a fallen tree for a seat he dug into his knapsack for a couple of oatmeal biscuits and some chocolate, which he washed down with a few gulps of water from his canteen. It was cold against his teeth, but felt good going down. Now, he thought, this is a recognizable place, so if I take note of the

tracks I make in the snow, I can find my way back here if I need to.
He didn't know if he was going towards the estate or not; he must
conceivably have traveled two or even three miles by now, so there
should be some signpost to *Yasnaya Polyana*, surely? Yet there was
nothing. And no-one.

He was not the type to panic, and he did have a good basic
navigational sense. The trouble was, there was so little that was
distinctive enough to take bearings from. As he walked his mind
turned to all sorts of irrelevancies – what his friends in London
would think of his foolishness, how warm the weather might be in
Brisbane at this moment, what made him undertake this crazy
mission in the first place. It was that he wanted to do something
exceptional, something expeditionary. To push himself out into the
world. In school his heroes had always been the great pioneers –
Blaxland, Wentworth, Sturt, Flinders. He'd spent almost a year in
England staying with friends of his family, and had made a few useful
contacts for future reference, but it was now time to go home. And
then he conceived of returning to Australia by this route – train
across Europe, a boat to Helsinki, the train again to Moscow, stay a
few days and then the long rail journey east across Siberia, and then
south to Japan. He knew from information gathered in London that
he would be able to catch a Japanese Mail Line steamer from
Yokohama to Brisbane. It had all seemed an irresistible challenge.
And then, lying in his bunk on the train out of Paris, reading the
Maude translation of *What is Art?* the thought came to him that since
he was going to be in Moscow for a few days he might take this
opportunity to meet the great man himself. He had run through how
it would be. Yes, he would go to *Yasnaya Polyana*, he would front up
to the house and proudly announce that he had come all the way
from Australia to meet the most wonderful writer alive. Surely he
would be impressed. Surely he would invite him in, offer him some
tea perhaps, a little something to eat. They would talk about The

Novel, about the similarities and differences between the Australian outback and the Russian plains, and the moral and economic importance of living close to the land. Perhaps he would be offered some pearls of wisdom, who knows? On the other hand, what if he was being foolish? What if they found nothing to say to each other, or worse he discovered just an ordinary human being after all, with petty hates and appetites like the rest of us, or a foul temper and a mean spirit? This is what one risks in getting too close to one's heroes. This is probably why he recoiled at the idea of reading biographies: it must inevitably diminish the hero's standing.

He really was feeling the cold now. While the effort of walking had the potential to warm him, it was not enough. Despite the woolen gloves, his fingers were starting to numb. His teeth were chattering, and when he tried to wipe the drip from his nose it actually snapped off on the back of his hand, a perfectly clear stalactite. And more snow falling again. He looked about him; it hardly mattered which direction he took, it was all one. He checked his watch; it had been over forty minutes since he left the station. That would have taken him at least two miles, surely. Possibly nearer three. He would surely have seen some indication of the Estate by this time, so obviously he had taken the wrong direction. Back to his tracks or he'd lose them altogether. But after a hundred yards or so, turning past a broad bush, he could no longer see them. All around was now an unmarked blanket of white. So he turned around again and resumed the direction he thought was right, but growing more convinced that he had already lost his way. Cold, tired, lonely and feeling an abject failure, he began to drop his head. Tears welled in his eyes, and his mouth tightened in bitterness: he knew in his heart he was about to fail.

And then he saw something strange. A lone figure, standing next to a tree, about three feet high, wearing an old brown cap and a red woolen scarf, not moving, not speaking, not alive. The body white, corpulent, the stumpy head neckless, molded into the sloping shoulders; an amputee, eyes of flint, and a cork between them, but no mouth. No need for a mouth if it couldn't speak. And if it could speak what would it say? In this other desert, in this bleached absence, there is no-one to address, nothing to come to mind, just the blank surround of nothingness. All thought of colour, of life, of movement, is about the past, that other country. The present, here, in this moment, gives nothing but emptiness. This is the not-life, the not-now; for life and a present that can sustain, one must reach only for the past. The future, that of course is useless, unknowable except for that real death it all comes down to. No, only the past is alive, and that is where one can be moved, laugh, hope, achieve. If I think of now, I am unhappy, I know that much. This little companion, this mute guard, has delivered the wisdom that I know I need.

He could make out the dark tip of a roof gable. He quickened his efforts, his spirits rising, and pushed harder through the fresh snow with aching calves and thighs. As he neared it he saw that it was certainly a large house of some kind, a white two-storey Georgian rectangle with rows of windows and a long driveway leading up to it. He could see no people moving about, but he optimistically put this down to the weather. In ten minutes he was trudging up to the front door of a country mansion probably a hundred years old. There was no name, nor anything to indicate the identity of the property. Was this it? Was this *Yasnaya Polyana*, Tolstoy's birthright, home, workplace? With a gloved hand he rapped on the central panel of the huge timber. Not only did the solid timber make hardly a sound, but his cold-stiffened knuckles pained from the blow. Using his metal water canteen, he knocked again, this time making enough noise to be heard at a distance inside. He waited.

He was nineteen years old. And though there was a maturity beyond his years in those handsome features, he was at heart boyish and in this country hopelessly out of his element. He was used to gazing across distances flooded with harsh sunlight, as the lightly etched crow's feet beside his eyes testified. Snow, cold of this depth, people with whom he could not communicate, were bewilderingly unfamiliar. He spoke a little French, but had no aptitude for languages (unlike my grandmother). Yet he was no peasant, no manual worker; anyone could tell from just a few minutes with him, noting that confident articulation, those alert eyes, the easy but delicate manners, that he was essentially a creature of the mind.

After several minutes there was still no answer to his knock. He went back down the steps and began the long trek to the end of the house and round the back. There was farm machinery, outbuildings, yards for animals with some horses, and in the distance a few people who looked like peasants moving about, and beyond them fields that were clearly part of the estate. Should he try asking them if he was in the right place? He was pessimistic, both about his ability to make himself understood, and about their answers. He looked over the back of the house, and still there was no sign of life. Clearly there was no-one inside. But shouldn't he at least go up one of the workers and find out if this was in fact *Yasnaya Polyana*? And here was the crucial thing. Now that the first wave of disappointment had run through him, he couldn't find it in his heart to fight back; he was giving in to the inevitable, that after all this effort coming all this way, his determination was abandoning him. Time was running out, too; he looked at his pocket watch and saw that it was coming up to 2.00 pm. It was almost three hours since he got off the train; it would take him another three hours to get back, providing he didn't get lost. Still, he might at least try to ascertain how close to his goal he had come. He began to trudge through the dirty snow and ice of the yard across towards the figures near the distant buildings, waving an arm to catch someone's attention. A long-bearded man wearing a heavy grey frock and a type of train driver's blue hat turned from what he was doing and stared straight at the approaching stranger. He stopped within ten metres of the peasant and said '*Yasnaya Polyana?*' The peasant didn't move, or reply. He repeated the question. The peasant said nothing. He took a few more paces towards him, and suddenly the peasant reacted. Bending quickly to his left, he came up with a long-handled pitchfork, and held it at the ready. The young man held up his hands in appeasement, and started talking:

'Easy, easy old fella – I just want to know if this is the estate of Count Leo Tolstoy. Is this where I am ? *Yasnaya Polyana?*'

The peasant for a moment didn't move, and said nothing. But with the pitchfork he gestured back towards the yard and the road leading into it, clearly demanding that he go back to where he came from. Then he spoke:

'*Net, Net. Net.*'

'Are you saying this is not *Yasnaya Polyana?* Is that what you mean by saying 'no'?'

The peasant took a couple of steps towards him, again brandishing the fork in a way that made it clear he did not want to engage with him, and wanted him to clear off. He saw that it was hopeless. He was going to get nothing out of the man, and nothing out of his attempts to find out where he was. And so he turned his back and abjectly retraced his steps to the front of the house, casting about for any sign of a name, a plaque, any indication of the identity of the property. Nothing. He stood for several minutes trying to come to terms with the situation. It was maddening. It was a conspiracy against his hopes. And now time was against him. He tried to rehearse all the plans he had built up along the way, but he quickly saw that this would only increase his disappointment, twist the knife of failure in his breast one more time. And that was the truth of the matter: failure. It was a new experience in his young life. An unexpected one, but one he might yet have to get used to.

He picked up his knapsack, slung it over his shoulder, and

doggedly began the long trek away from the house and back to the station. The snow had stopped falling, his boots sank into the powdery build up along the roadway, which, in the clear air, he could now make out as it ran between two tall blocks of forest ahead. But the sun was still refusing to come out, and the dark grey clouds up ahead were suggesting that more snow would fall before he reached the station. He tried to walk faster, but it was slow going in the powdery snow, and time seemed to have evaporated; the next pause he took showed it had passed four o'clock already.

As he trudged on he eventually recognized the barn he'd briefly sheltered in on his way from the station, coming into view now on his left. He couldn't see the horse. It wasn't near the fence where he had tossed the hay bale, and he couldn't see any hay either; it must have eaten it all. He knew he should be hurrying on, but a pang of sympathy prompted him to go over and maybe toss another bale over the fence. When he got there the horse was still not in sight. There were a few scraps of the hay left scattered in clumps on the slushy ground beside the fence. Still, he thought, no harm in giving him another bale, and he made his way towards the barn. Entering the wide-open doorway, he was surprised to see the horse inside, feasting on a broken-up hay bale, that looked like it had fallen, or been pulled from the small stack. 'Hello there old fella,' he laughed, 'how did you get in here?' The horse went on nonchalantly munching, but this in itself he took to be a sign of friendly acceptance on its part; it wasn't in any way alarmed at his arrival. He reached up and ran his hand along its back and withers, which felt warm and strong under his palm, then down the sloping neck, which caused the animal to stop eating, lift and turn its head in his direction. He ran his hand lightly down its forehead and fondled the muzzle, which he well knew horses liked. They both stood there for a few minutes, horse and man, lost in the momentary pleasure of contact, until it suddenly hit him. 'My god, the train, I have to get moving!'

He shouldered his rucksack, headed for the doorway, then stopped and took out his watch to attempt a quick calculation of how far and how much time he might have to get to the station. It was almost 4.45pm. Given that the carriage had brought him most of the way to this point, he reckoned it would take at least forty-five minutes walking back from here, and the train left at 5.20. He wouldn't make it. But he was a good man in a crisis, a practical man; whenever he found himself in need of solutions his brain stepped up its activity, and he usually found a way out. And so it was this time. He turned back and looked straight at the horse, cast about for a saddle, but of course there was none – it was a cart horse, not a show horse – but he did spot a bridle and reins hanging near the entrance. And farther back in the barn stood the dray, its weathered shafts resting on the earthen floor. But when he went closer to examine it he saw that it was missing it's left rear wheel. No good. He would have to ride, and bareback too. It took him only a couple of minutes to work out how to fit the bridle, bit and reins, which were too long of course, but that was no matter. The animal stood calm and expectant while the gear was fitted. Still wearing his knapsack, he hurled himself chest-first up onto the horse's back, swung his legs around so he was sitting right, took up the slack on the reins, and with a light kick of his heels on the bulging flanks, they trotted out of the barn. The horse snorted approvingly, clearly pleased to be out and moving, and once they got on the road it willingly took up a steady canter.

He had of course ridden bareback many times before back home, but nothing quite as high and broad-backed as a draught horse. His legs were splayed a little painfully, and his knees especially were rubbing against the rough-coated flanks; they would be sore that night. But the height was wonderful, enabling him to see farther, and to feel slightly grand as they began to pass farmhouses within sight of the road. In fact he felt a little kingly, a little privileged, when a small group of peasants on the side of the road followed him with wary eyes as he rode past. He hoped none of them recognized the horse, but he could see they were so taken with this foreigner's appearance that they didn't notice his mount. There was little on the road apart from a couple of carts heading in the opposite direction, and the horse was able to keep up a nice, steady gait, so they made good time.

The road led directly into the village, and when he came to it he remembered the only turn he had to make, which was a right, where the roadway branched to run alongside the railway line, off the main road only a few hundred yards from the station. He slid down the left flank, led the horse over to a little area off the road where he tied the reins to a small tree, and kicked away enough snow from the ground to expose about a square metre or two of deadish grass. The horse immediately bent to feed. 'Goodbye old boy,' he said into its twitching ear, 'you certainly saved my arse, if not my life.' He gave a final pat of appreciation, and crossed the road to the station.

The train was at the platform, the huge black engine hissing clouds of white steam. Doors and steps on the dark red carriages were clattering as a few people farther along were boarding with luggage and boxes. As he hurried along looking for a suitable compartment he passed a man in dark overalls tapping the wheels of the carriages with a little metal hammer, and making a quiet humming noise that sounded happy, though by the sour look on his face he might have been the unhappiest man in Russia. Tap, tap, tap went the ring of the hammer, and he recalled immediately the reference and what it meant. His emotions suddenly went into a riot of confusion – of disappointment, of understanding, of shame and, somewhere in his young heart as if it would burst, of sheer pride. With a lump in his throat and a well of tears in his eyes he found a step and boarded, ignored the first few compartments containing people, and threw himself into the first empty seat he came to. The knapksack up on the rack, he sat and tossed back his head, closed his eyes, and waited, waited, till the sound of the train bell and the lurch of the carriage brought him back to the world about him. His heart was still pounding. It wasn't until they'd been travelling some twenty minutes that his breathing had slowed, his body had relaxed, his mind had calmed enough for him to stand up, take a book from his rucksack, and begin to read, yet again, his copy of *What Is Art?* He was happier now, reconciled now. When the ticket inspector came along he asked how long it would be till they got to Moscow. The inspector looked out of the window and circumspectly at the sky, and began to nod his approval, as if affirming that there seemed to be no further storms in sight. He straightened and held up four pudgy fingers in the face of the young man.

Trade

During the last years of the Second World War, after we'd moved from the city to the country town of Mount Macedon, my father often promised to take me hunting for rabbits. Finally, on a particularly sunny Saturday morning, we were sitting on the front veranda when, in front of my mother, he decided to make good his promise, and take me out rabbiting the following day. 'It'd do you good to get out, both of you, if was a nice day like today; and who knows,' she laughed, 'we might end up with bunny for dinner.' There were two problems standing in the way: his tuberculosis, which made it difficult for him to walk long distances, and the fact that we didn't own a gun. That first problem was a threat constantly keeping him apart from me; his infectiousness meant I couldn't go into his bedroom, couldn't hug or kiss him, and at times when the fever came on I was not even able to talk to him. It was only in the outdoors that we could be together. The effect was to intensify my desire to be in his presence, and fiercely idolize everything about him. He was beautiful in that other-worldly way that tubercular people can be, with his blonde hair and burning blue eyes, and flushed fair skin stretched over his raw young cheekbones and chin. And to my mind he was always wise and clever, sketching in bed or making soft toys with macrame and coloured felt. Any chance of my spending a whole afternoon by his side, having him entirely to myself, was a glimpse of paradise.

The second problem, my mother managed to solve that week by some quick thinking. She worked part-time behind the bar at the local pub, and so was regularly in conversation with the men who drifted in late in the afternoons. Some were not locals, like the three painters from Bendigo who had been around for weeks sprucing up

Cameron Lodge, or the young baker who had, like us, recently moved up from Melbourne; in fact he took a room in our house as a boarder. He couldn't have been more than nineteen, and I remember his handsome features as he sat across the table from me in his navy roll-neck sweater, bolting down my mother's cooking with an alacrity I, as a picky nine-year-old, couldn't duplicate. The only food I really liked at that time was spaghetti with grated cheddar cheese; we'd never heard of bolognese or carbonara, but I could put away the plain stuff till I was fit to burst.

To get back to the gun, among the regulars at the pub was a noisy barfly, Brian Smith, who had boasted more than once of his prowess with a .22 rifle and the regularity with which he was able to feed his children on rabbit stew. It was during his latest bit of swagger that my mother hit on the idea of asking him if he would lend the gun to us for a day or so sometime soon.

'Anything for a beautiful girl like you Evelyn; I'll bring it in at the end of the week. Then you can give me a kiss to pay for it.'

My mother was not happy being in Smith's debt, as she often told us. She would sense his eyes ogling her as she reached up to the overhead rack for glasses, and was uncomfortable at the way he would inject a suggestive note into his talk.

'Frank?' he would say to her, 'that's your old man's name isn't it? Must be hard on a young woman like you, him being an invalid? Anytime you need anything, sweetheart, you just say the word. I'll be round like a shot.' And more than once, fishing for sympathy after his third or fourth beer, he had complained to her how his own wife had gone off with another man, leaving him with their three children. Money and a good time, he said, was all women wanted.

'If you haven't got the dough, they never want to know,' he chanted across the bar. My mother did have some sympathy for him, and found it disturbing that a woman could abandon her children like that, but on the other hand she could understand anyone finding

Smith difficult to live with. At first glance he was good-looking —
dark eyebrows, athletic in a stringy kind of way, except that he had a
way of hunching his shoulders that made him appear shifty. And
when he opened his mouth a junkyard of rotting teeth reminded you
that he chain-smoked and stank. He had a habit of hawking gobbets
of phlegm from behind his nose, strolling to the pub door and
dobbing them onto the pathway, where of course people walked.

The publican had warned my mother not to give Smith any
credit. 'He still owes me twenty quid from last Christmas, when I was
stupid enough to feel sorry for him. Well, for the kids really. I told
him to buy them something nice, seeing their mother had gone off
like that, but I know he used it to buy that rifle from a bloke in
Woodend. When I questioned him about it, he said the kids would
benefit more from that than some tin rubbish made in Japan — it
would put food on the table.'

'Does he have a job?' my mother asked.

'He says he used to own a wood yard in Gisborne before the
War, but all he does now is bludge off the government. Child
endowment. He rents a place down along Hanson's Road. He's a
battler, I know, but if I let him put it on the tab he'll never pay it. So
you tell him its cash or no grog.'

At the dinner table my mother told all this to us.

'Now that was very smart of you to ask about the gun', said
my father, and added in his best mock-diffidence, 'Of course it helps
to have looks like Vivien Leigh.'

'Oh yes, smarty pants,' she said, pulling a face at him, 'it's a
shame then that I don't have Clark Gable to come home to, isn't it.'

'Who's Clark Gable?' I asked.

'The man in the moon,' said my mother.

'Oh, and yes', said my father, 'I'll get you to pick up a packet
of bullets from Greenbaum's store on your way home tomorrow
night.'

'Can you get me a comic, too?' I asked, seizing my opportunity.

The timing of the loan was fortunate, because it was one of the few occasions when my father was well enough to go out beyond the veranda of our house; he had been up and around that week, dressed thankfully in normal clothes rather than the pyjamas and burgundy dressing gown that always so depressed me. As is well known, tuberculosis of the lung not only makes it hard to breathe, but it is also unpredictable; it can suddenly improve to the point where strength returns almost to normal. Just as quickly, fits of coughing and high fever can recur, and the sufferer is confined to bed for many days. My father spent a lot of time in this state, shut in the bedroom away from the rest of us, trying to ensure that my mother, my younger brother or I weren't infected. He also had, despite being only in his early thirties, an old-fashioned view that illness was essentially a private matter, and that it was indecent to display your infirmities to the world at large. So I never saw the blood-spitting, the delerium, the clawing for breath, until the very end.

It is hardly surprising, then, that I was beside myself with happiness that morning on the veranda at the prospect of him keeping his promise at last to take me out after those rabbits he had so often talked about. My mother had brought the rifle home on the Friday night, wrapped in brown paper and tied with string. As my father unwrapped it, it seemed a thing of seductive power and beauty with its polished wooden stock and black metal barrel. He took from the kitchen drawer a small box of cartridges, which I picked up and scrutinised; *Made in Czechoslovakia*, it said. My father took out the rifle bolt and cleaned the breach and barrel with an oily rag and some string. 'A long time since that was done.' he said, and then with some solemnity, 'Remember, you must never point a gun at a person, even if it is not loaded,' a piece of advice I've always taken seriously.

We left early on that fresh, sunny Sunday morning. Mother put some sweet biscuits in a bag in my trouser pocket, and made my father and me wear the Fair Isle jumpers she had knitted for us to wear in that cold mountain climate during winter. We walked a route down and away from the mountain looming over us, through the high-grass of biscuit-brown paddocks stretching away before us, along deep gullies, amongst scrubby clumps of sweet-smelling eucalypt. I was allowed to carry the rifle, which my father reminded me to handle safely, keeping it loaded but with the bolt on safety. There weren't many rabbits about. Occasionally we saw movements on distant slopes, but not close enough to take a shot. To answer his need for action, my father took a few shots at crows, missing them all. 'Crows always know to move off just as you pull the trigger,' he said. Once, he placed an old jam tin on a fence post and put a couple of shots through that, 'Just to get my eye in', he said. He was enjoying himself, and, I noticed, hadn't coughed once.

Walking along a dry creek bed, we came upon a scattering of rabbits capering in different directions, their white tails bobbing up the steep slope. My father gave a looping whistle as if he was calling a dog, and one of the rabbits paused at the top of the slope, the outline of ears clear against the blue sky. I held my breath while he aimed, the rifle cracked, and the rabbit rolled back down the slope. 'Go and get 'im', said my father. When I picked it up by the leg and held it by the back its soft fur was warm and supple, but marked in the neck with a dark bloodstain. For a moment I regretted what had happened, but the feeling quickly passed when my father said cheerfully, 'That'll do just nicely for tea tonight,' and emptying the magazine into his cupped hand, he put the remaining bullets in his pocket. Opening his white-handled pocket knife he cut a slit in one of the rabbit's back legs, and pushed the other leg through it, so that it formed a handle for carrying. That was my job.

We didn't go straight home. 'Might as well to return the gun to Mr. Smith,' said my father, 'seeing we're not all that far from where he lives.' We stumped along for what seemed ages, and after a while I noticed him breathing more heavily. 'A bit further than I thought,' he laughed, but I began to worry. We kept going until we got to a flat area where there was a decrepit-looking weatherboard house set back from the dirt road; around it was nothing but bare, dusty paddock, not a tree nor a flower. I couldn't help comparing it to the wild garden around our house, full of good climbing trees and bushes ideal for hideaways, and was glad we didn't live in this place. My father knocked on the door, and after a few minutes it was opened by a slim man wearing a grubby waistcoat over his even grubbier white shirt, and a battered grey hat like most men wore.

'Brian. Frank Mahon. This is my boy, Vinnie.'

'Frank', he beamed a smile full of bad teeth as they shook hands, 'I see you got one, then. Biggie too.'

'Returning your property,' said my father, handing him the rifle, 'and thank you, very good of you to let us have it. Yeah, we'll be having nice fresh bunny for tea.'

'Listen', said Smith, 'come in and have a beer with me. Got a cold bottle in the ice chest.'

'Ooh, I dunno,' said my father, 'it's a bit early…'

'Aw, go on – it's comen' up to lunch time; give y'an appetite.'

'Well, as a matter of fact I could do with a sit down for few minutes; the walk's been a bit tougher than I expected.'

I guessed my father also felt obliged to him, and uncomfortable at the idea of turning him down, so after he found a nail in the veranda post to hang our rabbit on, we went inside. There were several big-eyed children in an untidy lounge room with only a single old brown armchair for furniture. There was also a distinctive smell; I came to know that smell only too well in subsequent years, when things took a turn for the worse in our family; it is the smell of staleness, of clothes worn too long without washing, of blocked drains and unclean houses; the smell of poverty and all that goes with it. The Smith children, of various sizes, grubby and silent, staring at us with blank expressions, were my first taste of this special brand of misery.

My father and Smith went into the gloomy kitchen, sat up to the table on bare wooden chairs, and talked while they drank their beer from familiar pub glasses. My father commented on them, and how it is always good to drink cold beer from a tall glass.

'Well,' laughed Smith, 'Glover's not gunna miss 'em, izzy?' I was alert enough at that age to know that the glasses had been stolen from the pub. Then unexpectedly he said to the biggest girl, 'Deirdre, take Vinnie and show him the dog, And the rest of you kids go out too, and play in the yard.'

Suddenly, bewildering things happened. Deirdre, maybe two years older than I, grabbed my hand and pulled me out and down the back steps into the dusty yard. Across the dry grass a faded brown dog, almost the same colour as the dust it lay on, was chained to a woodshed. The two smaller children, a boy and a girl, followed, silent. I went over to pat the dog, but when it bared its teeth and growled I thought better of it. Then the girl dragged me round to the side of the woodshed, out of sight of the house. I remembered then that I'd seen her in the play-ground at school once or twice, among some of the older kids. She pushed me up against the wire fence.

'Have you got anything?' she demanded.

'What do you mean?'

'Have you got anything? There, in your pocket. Money?'

'No.'

I felt in my pocket and took out the bag of biscuits to show to her, thinking I might offer her one. She snapped at the other children, 'Buzz off, go and play round the front.' They hesitated for a moment, then ran off. Deirdre stepped closer; she was a good bit taller than me, and looked down coldly into my face.

'Give me them,' she said, 'and I'll let you do anything you like to me.'

I froze with ignorance. What did she mean? What could I do to her? She meant something that I didn't understand. Her hands went under her light dress, and quickly slipped down her navy pants; she stepped out of them and hung them over the fence.

'Here,' she said, lifting her dress, 'do what you want,' and she grabbed the bag of biscuits from my hand. Taking her words as an order, her theft as a settled exchange, I obediently examined her. I had never seen how a girl is made before, having seen only myself and my little brother in the bath. I was surprised that there was nothing to see but a cleft, and a light smattering of fuzz. I reached out and tentatively touched its firm softness where it protruded a little, with her legs pressed together. When I looked up and searched her face for some sort of response, she was gazing impassively into the distance, contentedly devouring the biscuits. Suddenly, she opened her legs. I pulled away as if I'd been bitten.

'Okay,' I said, 'thank you.'

'Is that all you want to do?' she asked, 'Don't you want to put it up?'

'No.' I said quickly. 'Up where? What?'

'You know, your finger, up properly?'

I couldn't quite grasp what she meant, or the purpose of it. 'No, it's okay. That's all I want to do,' I said; it seemed important not to appear ignorant.

She put her pants back on and laughed at me. 'You're so stupid,' she said, and ran to the back steps.

'Are there any biscuits left?' I called after her.

'There you are,' she laughed, and threw the crushed-up empty bag at me. Then she disappeared inside. All I could think to do was sit around on the back step and wait for the men to finish their beer and their talk, and for us to be on our way.

When we left, my father remembered to fetch the rabbit from the veranda, and gave it to me to carry. I had to keep shaking the flies off it. Walking back a different way from the way we came, along the road this time, I was hungry and looking forward to getting home for lunch. My father, who had stayed quiet for some time, brooding on something, finally spoke up:

'Brian Smith is a sad feller.'

I guessed he meant something more than that, but I choose to take him literally.

'Is he sad because he doesn't have any garden around his house?' I said.

He put his arm round my shoulder. 'Mate,' he said, 'that man doesn't have anything except his kids.'

'He's got a gun,' I said.

'True, he's got a gun. But he hasn't got a job, and he hasn't got a wife, and the kids haven't got a mother. A sad feller.'

'He's got a dog,' I said.

'That's right, he has. Did Deirdre show you the dog? What did you do out there?'

The question struck me into silence. What we did out there was almost nothing, and yet I couldn't bring myself to speak of it. Shame, and guilt, and confusion demanded it remain unmentioned. I knew I was blushing, but thankfully he didn't notice. I kept thinking about Deirdre, and often thought about her for weeks, and even years afterwards, as the keeper of dark adult secrets, of forbidden acts that were full of danger, not just to anyone who wanted to enter that world, but to herself, that there was much bluff in her cold smugness, and that everything about her life was wrong – the smells in that motherless house, the lack of furniture, the dusty, treeless backyard with its cur chained to the shed, and most of all Smith himself, her father, with his bad teeth and stink and the way his scrawny body angled into a fixed gesture of defeat and his thin voice never seeming to mean what it said – and I felt a great rush of pity for her.

'I gave her my biscuits,' I said.

'Well, that was generous of you,' he said, 'I hope she shared them with the others. I guess you must be getting hungry.'

By the time we got home he was having great trouble in breathing, and was so exhausted from the long walk that he went straight to bed. He wasn't even able to eat any of the rabbit casserole my mother made for dinner that night. With my brother asleep in his cot on the other side of the room, I was reading my *Felix the Cat* comic in bed, when from way down the hall I heard my mother yell 'Frank! Frank!' There was something in her voice that struck at my heart – a note of deep terror, and not just immediate but a terror that had been building up in her for many months, in her worry over money, in her frustrations over our leaky roof, in her anxiety over my father's worsening health, in the very state of living that we had been struggling against – and it tore me out of bed and dragged me in a rush down the hall towards the kitchen. Then halfway down the hall my father was lying on the floor in the doorway to his bedroom, in his pyjamas, unconscious. My mother was standing over him, her arms covered in soap suds, held out in a gesture of helplessness. Her eyes were wild and frightened. But my appearance seemed to trigger her into action.

'I'm going to the hotel to phone for the doctor – stay with daddy till I get back. I won't be long…'

I sat down on the floor next to him; his face was burning hot, and he was very still. I reached out with my hand to give his shoulder the occasional stroke.

The doctor eventually came, by which time he had regained consciousness and my mother had helped him back into bed. For a long time the doctor talked to my mother in the bedroom in low voices, and when he was leaving she walked him onto the front veranda, where they continued talking. I could tell it was important, and heard the doctor say 'no more walking'. I quietly tiptoed along the hall. Standing in the doorway of his bedroom I watched him propped up on his bank of pillows, his head back and blue eyes staring at the ceiling, as if they would burn holes in it. 'Frank,' I whispered to myself, and the name echoed through the hall and in my head, and on down the years, through my teens and into adult life, as it still does; it's a name I have revered all my life.

The White Koala

'it is racism that gives rise to race, never the other way around.'
Andreas Malm

Gina was the first to admit that she was not an educated woman, though she had always been an avid reader, especially of novels. She preferred them to have a romantic interest, to be what she considered well-written, and preferably recommended by someone whose opinion she trusted, such as her daughter or a close friend. Her reasons for joining the 'Literature for Pleasure' class of the University of the Third Age, or U3A as everyone calls it, an organization that runs courses for retirees, were therefore partly intellectual; she certainly enjoyed talking about books. But she also wanted to make new friends, to improve her social life at least a little, and perhaps find someone who could offer her something that was more than friendship; since her divorce four years earlier there had been no one. She believed she was still attractive, and even if a little plumpish here and there, had at least managed to avoid wrinkles, and she took special pride in her girlishly smooth neck. After thirty-two years of marriage she disliked sleeping alone; she missed the comforting attentions of a man. She would never dream of approaching a dating agency, or actively looking for one, yet always managed to convey the message that she was definitely open to the possibility.

The man she liked most was Tom Griffith, the class tutor. Tall, deep-voiced, a shock of unkempt white hair and matching beard, Tom possessed a solid masculinity reinforced by forthright opinions and a cheerful nature. He had taught secondary school English from the time he left college until his retirement several years ago, and after a lifetime of Sisyphean classroom effort with bored teenagers he now basked in the flattery of attentive adults.

Theoretically, at least, Gina considered him available: she had heard him say once that his wife of forty years had died of cancer, and that he now lived alone in their house in Torquay. But to her disappointment Tom had so far shown no reciprocal interest in her; in fact he seemed, whenever she offered an opinion or asked a question, to treat her with an impatience bordering on contempt. On one occasion, during a class on *Pride and Prejudice*, she ventured the comment that some of the interpretations being expressed around her, particularly by the very opinionated Gerard Da Silva, would hardly have been intended by the author of the work herself. Tom smiled patronisingly, 'Gina, I'm sorry to tell you, but that approach is pretty naive and completely irrelevant; we can't know what the author *intended*, only what she *wrote*.' Chastised, she blushed and kept her mouth shut for the rest of the lesson.

Afterwards, when the others were preparing to leave, noting her embarrassment Gerard drew her aside and said, 'Don't take everything Tom says as gospel; he thinks he knows more than he does; in fact, the question of authorial intention is a very complex and much debated one, which I think we should take up at a later date. It's not as irrelevant as Tom makes out.'

Gerard was someone she definitely did not like, though she conceded he was clever and often said interesting things, especially when he talked about his growing up in Sri Lanka. But he would get into long, convoluted disputes with Tom, who usually insisted on the last word in the discussion, and Gina thought 'fair enough' – he was the tutor after all, and she was happy to see Gerard put in his place occasionally. Shortish, olive-skinned, pepper-and-salt-bearded and balding, in his sixties, he was probably still attractive to women, despite a certain sloppy corpulence. It was his manner she didn't like. He had the air of a man bent on persuasion – to his point of view on everything, persistent as a dog with a bone. Moreover, lately he seemed to have been 'coming on to her', as her daughter would have put it. And going by something Ann Lovett once said, he had a reputation for it.

Sotto voce, she replied to Gerard, 'I just wish people wouldn't go on so much with their theories and far-fetched interpretations. Can't we just enjoy the books for what they are?' Her gaze fixed on his generous, moist lips, which she imagined, with repulsion, kissing hers. As he spoke he laid a hand on her bare lower arm; touching was another of his habits she found uncomfortable. 'But we're here to *learn* something, Gina, not just to indulge ourselves in chat. Are you going for coffee?' Gina took her arm away and threw a glance at Tom, who was closing up his briefcase.

'Are you going for coffee Tom?'

'I thought I might,' he said cheerfully.

'Yes, okay,' said Gina, 'let's all go then.'

An ironical smile appeared on Gerard's face, giving her the huge satisfaction of realizing that the message she was trying to convey had managed to find its mark: Tom mattered, not him.

These after-class coffee sessions had acquired an importance in the early days of the class, when it was held in town. Every Tuesday afternoon at least six or seven of them had been accustomed to walk the short distance into the centre to enjoy the cozy, classy atmosphere of *The Loving Cup*, with its wonderful coffee aroma and its polished timber chairs and tables. The buzz of talk among its mostly middle-aged clients embraced you like a warm blanket the moment you opened the heavy glass door straight off the street. But when the U3A moved to premises next to a new shopping mall on the outskirts of town, suddenly the class lost its beloved cafe. No one liked this new area. It was flat and exposed, one of those developments done all-of-a-piece, with the houses, streets and shops all built by the same developer, quickly and, if the houses were anything to go by, pretty cheaply. But everyone understood that it provided affordable housing and facilities for young families; it just wasn't what you wanted once you were at their later stage of life. The class now had to find somewhere new to enjoy their coffee and post-mortems, and discreet probings into each other's lives.

It was actually Gina, on the day of the first class in the new building, who'd come up with news of a likely venue. She had a talent for keeping informed on any significant developments around town. At the south end of the shopping mall there had recently been built a detached complex comprising a medical centre, a tax agent's office, a TAB betting shop and a new cafe. Modest in size though the complex was, its cream stone Federation style buildings, landscaped surrounds with young crepe myrtles in stone planter boxes in the same style and color, had to Gina's eye an impressive 'retro' look, much superior to the rest of the mall. She suggested they give the cafe a try, and everyone agreed. It was called, she told them, *The White Koala*.

There were only four of them on this first visit – Gina, Tom, Gerard and Ann Lovett. Ann was something of a wonder. Small, freckled, lean as a stick and sharp-beaked, she had successfully raised seven children, and though she had a meagre formal education and had held only modest office jobs, she was a most intelligent and well-read member of the class; and she was always keen to go for coffee afterwards. They filed in, chatting happily, and settled upon one of the bigger tables at the back next to a plate glass window. The place was all spanking new, its carpeted floor and furniture all color-coordinated in smart pinks and greys, and completely empty. It didn't look like there had been a customer all day, or any other day for that matter. And no one seemed to be serving. These were not good signs. In its favor were the expansive proportions of the place, the chrome and fabric modern chairs and glass-topped tables neatly positioned across the room. In front of one wall, containing shelves of dangerously attractive cakes, was a long, curved showcase that morphed into a small counter beside a huge stainless steel Gaggia coffee machine, also brand new. With these gleaming appointments, the place had for Gina the sterile feel of an interior design magazine, destined to be photographed rather than used.

Eventually, a dark-haired man emerged, coming smiling towards them with his hands clasped in front of his chest. He wore dark trousers and a tieless white shirt with the top button undone, and his appearance was distinctive; they all immediately recognized him as Middle-Eastern.

'Good afternoon,' he said in a soft voice, 'what can I get you ladies and gentlemen?'

The accent confirmed the origins, as did the clipped black goatee and moustache, the well-defined eyebrows, the good white teeth contrasted against a skin that, exposed to the sun, would have quickly darkened to a rich olive. It was difficult to judge his age; the face looked under fifty, but his stoop suggested more, and together with the smile made him seem deferential. Even, Gina surmised as he nodded while taking their orders, a touch sycophantic; an Arab stereotype vaguely lurked behind this conjecture, which try as she might she could not quite banish from her thoughts.

In turn they gave him their orders, a mixture of different coffees and teas, together with a variety of requests for snacks — carrot cake, scones with jam and cream, jelly slice and, Gina's favourite, a wedge of spicy plum cake with a dollop of cream. All this the man took in without the aid of a notepad, as though listening to an anecdote, and responding with a soft 'yes, yes' and a slight wag of his head to each order. As he went behind the counter to prepare the beverages, Gina wondered how many he might get wrong, or forget.

Gerard, sitting back in his chair pursing his mouth in distaste, looked distinctly unimpressed with the place. Seated adjacent to the window, Tom and Ann gazed out across a flat paddock of wild, uncut grass. Beyond were the raw fences of recently built houses, brick and timber constructions all similar in style. 'They have such small blocks these says,' said Ann, voicing a disapproval that they all felt, not just about the housing development but also about the whole suburban area. Tom said, 'When I think of the unmade gardens, the stuffed supermarket trolleys, the gigantic mortgages, the ferrying of children to school, I thank God I don't have to go through all that again,' and Ann wholeheartedly agreed.

Still exercising Gina's mind was the man who had just taken their orders, his strange incongruity with this mostly Anglo-Celtic, semi-rural world of tradesmen with young families, wives with basic education; Australia as it has been for generations, its views on immigrants driven by tabloid morals. Only recently a large protest group had forced a neighboring council to deny a building application for a small Muslim primary school, every objection to which the local paper gave disgracefully biased prominence. For a civilized group such as themselves, sitting in the cafe, it was a risky topic to broach, and so they remained silent on the subject just as they remained silent now about this man himself, even though Gina guessed he was very much on all their minds. They searched instead for the things that *could* be talked about.

'Bloody awful name for a café,' said Gerard.

'What is it?' said Tom, 'I didn't see.'

'*The White Koala*. It's written on the window as you come in.'

'Yuk, really?' said Ann, 'surely they could come up with something better than that.'

The man eventually appeared from the kitchen carrying a tray, and without needing to check with them, deftly placed the correct order with absolute accuracy before each of them. They each in turn said a firm 'thankyou' and waited in silence, staring at their order. Gina was astonished, not to say impressed. There was a sense that an icebreaker was needed, and Tom, who usually took the initiative, obliged. He addressed the man.

'I take it you've just opened the business, hoping to attract some regular customers?'

'Yeees, of course,' the man replied, still smiling, 'I expect it will be quiet for a little time, but I am hoping it will pick up before too long.' His tone was unhurried, reassuring.

Suddenly Tom shot out his right hand. 'Tom Griffith,' he said. For an instant the man looked startled, but immediately produced that smile and nod of the head in acceptance of the offer, grasping only the ends of Tom's fingers, and with more delicacy than vigor.

'Thank you,' he replied, 'my name is Ahmed. Enjoy your refreshments.' He tactfully placed the bill on the corner of the table, and went back behind the counter.

Tom's personal touch had worked, and the forces of discomfort felt that much weaker now. From this time on the group looked forward to a kind of solidarity with this man, this Ahmed, because overriding all their many assumptions and speculations about his background, about his choice to start a business in this of all areas, his acumen in finding the resources, his courageous leap of commercial faith, they sensed the brutal certainty that in this part of the world his cafe was surely doomed utterly to fail.

The class made *The White Koala* its regular Tuesday afternoon haunt. They got over their initial hesitations, and now took the place for granted. As usual their discussions were noisy and incomprehensible to anyone other than themselves, but it was obvious that they enjoyed it. Ahmed got to know names, and would even anticipate some of their orders. 'The usual, Tom – flat white?' he would say, or 'Any cake for you today Gina?' Some days they would exchange words about the weather, or the success of the local football team, always in the news. Ahmed usually kept himself informed enough to say something of interest. To add to their pleasure, Ahmed's coffee was excellent. 'We use only the best Colombian Arabica,' he told them, holding up his hands with thumbs and forefingers pressed together.

But there remained the unspoken fact of the pitiful custom that the café was attracting. What was strange about this was that the car park was crowded; it was getting harder every week to find a spot. Clearly the medical centre was doing great business, and probably the tax agent as well. And a women's hair salon had opened in the last remaining shop space since they first started going there. The TAB was prospering on the spoils from its optimistic regulars. But in the café there were never more than a few, maybe a couple of young mothers with children, a traveling salesman, but hardly enough to keep a business afloat. The group felt increasingly sorry for Ahmed, even at times angry at what they guessed was the reason. They surmised that surely his job must be at risk once the proprietors understood that reason. Yet they were also pleased with themselves; they were not part of that reason, they were happy to see their Tuesday afternoon custom as a positive resistance to the ugly spirit behind that reason.

But on one occasion that self-satisfaction received a shaking. Gina had often watched in admiration as he busied himself alone behind the counter, still not busy enough to need help, and wondered about him as he passed hour after lonely hour every day, gazing out the window, in this surely disheartening situation. She was prompted, consequently, when he was clearing the table this afternoon, to say, with the best of intentions and a genuine desire to know, about his 'gift' for being a waiter.

'Did you do a hospitality course somewhere in Melbourne, or were you a waiter back in your own country?'

Ahmed looked at her with a puzzled expression, and then with a cold frown that cut into her self-regard like a knife, before he unsmilingly replied, 'A course? Waiter? My own country? No Gina; this is my country. I am an Australian citizen. And I have never done a hospitality course.'

And then after bowing politely and taking a step or two back,

Ahmed turned and disappeared back into the kitchen. Gina did not know where to look. The others were silent, and did not engage with Gina's search for eye contact. Except for Gerard, who sat back in his chair and directed towards her a wry, dimpled, smug and smiling gaze.

As was his custom every year, Tom took Term 3 off from teaching the class. U3A, being an entirely voluntary organization, always allowed its tutors to make whatever arrangements suited them for the running of their courses. His class members always good-naturedly complained. 'What are we going to do with ourselves for three months while you're away?' Gina said, and they all did whatever they could to fill in their Tuesdays until the final Term and Tom's return. In the past some of them had booked holidays, and Tom usually went somewhere either on his own or with friends on some pursuit or other. Only this year, when he was asked, he said he had 'other things' to attend to, without feeling the need to explain himself further. When they all came back for Term 4 they spent half their first class chatting noisily about things that had happened in the interim – the U.S. election, changes in the fortunes of their AFL teams, the usual local political scandals and hypocrisies. They were all beside themselves with pleasure to be back in class, and eager to tackle the weekly topics that Tom had prepared for them.

Naturally, the regular after-class coffee time resumed at the cafe. Gerard continued his fruitless pursuit of Gina, while Tom meanwhile ignored all Gina's efforts to ensnare him. The weeks flew by, until it seemed there was almost no time left till the end of Term, and Christmas was approaching. To celebrate her birthday on November the 11th (Armistice Day had always given her celebrations a touch of dignity) Gina invited some of the class to her unit for lunch one Saturday – Tom, Ann, Carole Pinchbeck, Michael Morgan, and, surprising herself (she put it down to the Christmas spirit) – Gerard. But Tom gave his apologies; she was so disappointed. The lunch went off well enough, and almost inevitably since he was absent, the talk got around to Tom. Everyone liked him, it was obvious, even Gerard, despite their quarrels over literary theory and a clear resentment at Tom's popularity and successful exercise of authority on literary matters. But then Gerard said something across the table that shocked Gina : 'He hasn't been quite his affable self since his operation. That's what he was doing during his break – he told me about it when I ran in to him in the supermarket.'

'Operation?' she asked.

'Prostate. It hit him hard.'

'Did they catch it early?' asked Carole.

'Well, yes, but that hardly matters; what matters is the after-effect…' They watched as Gerard's mouth turned into almost a leer when he said this. Gina knew exactly what he meant, and she guessed he knew she knew. Nevertheless, he insisted on driving home the nail. 'No sex,' he said, with grey eyes fixed straight at Gina. 'He told me himself,' Gerard added: 'that part of his life is now over.' She didn't know what to say, so she got up from the table and pretended to busy herself at something in the kitchen. She knew she never hated Gerard more than in that moment. She had to stop herself from rushing out into the garden and screaming. Later in the afternoon, after everyone had left, her anger returned with the realisation that Tom must have told Gerard about his operation in confidence, and that Gerard had betrayed that confidence. She swore that she would never invite him to her place again.

The following Tuesday was the final class for the year, and after an enjoyable couple of hours tearing apart *Huckleberry Finn*, the class – every one of them this time – removed to Ahmed's, as they had now taken to calling the café (*White Koala* indeed!) for their last get-together before Christmas. Ahmed had hung gold and silver balls around the café, and placed a gaudily decorated and lit plastic imitation of a tree in a corner. They were so many that they had to push together two large tables, and drag chairs around to get everyone seated. Gina noted with some surprise, and pointed out to Tom, that a couple of new staff were working in the place – a tall, overweight young red-haired man and a pretty young Filipina. But then again, Tom pointed out, the numbers of customers had been increasing over recent weeks, so business must be improving. Still, it was quiet on this Tuesday afternoon; the only customers in the café were themselves, apart from a man in overalls reading a newspaper at a table near the door. Gina looked for Ahmed, and with some relief saw him emerge from the small kitchen behind the counter. She was tempted to wave, but he became involved in talking to the red-haired young man.

The Filipina came over to take their orders, and after much confusion and repetition, the inexperienced girl eventually managed to get it all written down. They were all so busy talking that they hardly noticed the long interval until she re-emerged from the kitchen carrying a cluttered tray. Moving towards them with an unsteadiness that suggested the floor might give way under her, she arrived at their table and distributed the choices, but not before making several mistakes, repeating the confusion that obtained when she was writing them down, and prompting a havoc of exchanges that took several minutes to complete. When all cups were finally before their rightful owners, she straightened up and rewarded them all with a beatific smile on her pretty face. Ahmed came across to them, with the red-haired giant trailing sluggishly behind him.

'Good afternoon ladies and gentlemen,' he began in his typically formal style, 'I hope you had a rewarding class today. I have something I wish to say: regretfully I have to tell you that this is the last time I will be serving you here in the *The White Koala*; from today you will have Gary here to look after you, and of course his lovely wife Corazon.'

Unexpected as it was, it took barely a moment for everyone to realize that this should come as no surprise. But they still found it sad. This is what happens when the forces of darkness prevail. This is a story only too common throughout the State, indeed throughout the country, they had no doubt. What would Ahmed do now? Gina wondered; what will he do for an income? Centrelink, she supposed.

'Giving up? Not able to put up with it any longer, Ahmed?' Tom's tactlessly cheerful tone made Gina wince. Ahmed nodded graciously to him.

'No, no Tom, nothing like that; Gary here is taking up the lease, that is all. And I will be moving to where I have another business to establish. But I might see you when I come back to attend to a few matters from time to time. You see…'

At this point red-haired Gary, obviously bored, gave them all a cursory wave of his fingers, yawned and walked back to the counter, leaving Ahmed to continue his explanation.

'… I own this complex, and I have to keep an eye on the landscaping, the maintenance and so on. So, I will be coming around from time to time…'

Everyone at the table froze, looking directly at Ahmed, who was not smiling now, but talking soberly, as one who had come at last to a subject that required his serious attention, and that he was only too happy to confide to the group.

'You *own* it all?' said Tom, with undisguised astonishment.

'Yes, yes – the whole complex – the medical centre, the TAB, everything. You see, I had to get the café – the business – up and running so I could lease it more easily; now I'm going to do the same with another place I own on the other side of town. This is what I do, and it often allows me to meet wonderful people like all of you. So, thank you for the opportunity, and I wish you all a very happy Christmas, and hope that you continue to enjoy your literature classes.'

Gina looked at Tom. Tom looked at Gerard. Gerard looked at Ann. Ann looked at Gina. And they all shook their heads and laughed. And Ahmed joined in and laughed with them.

'This makes you all happy, yes?' he said.

'Well, we'll miss you, but it makes us all very happy.' said Tom, 'and a Merry Xmas to you too, Ahmed.'

But though she was still laughing with the rest, Gina was experiencing a little stab of doubt. She was not so sure she *ought* to be happy with the news.

When U3A classes resumed the following February, Gina, Tom, Ann and Gerard agreed to see if it was worth continuing to frequent *The White Koala*, under its new management. When they arrived they couldn't find a nearby parking spot, they had to leave their cars further away, in the supermarket car park, and walk. When they got there, the cafe was packed with customers. It was so hard to find a seat that they ended up squashed into a corner at a small table. Red-haired Gary and lovely Corazon were run off their feet attending to tables, and apparently they had someone working in the kitchen. Corazon sang across the room to them, 'I'll come for your orders soon,' but she was so busy it clearly was not going to be soon, or soon enough.

Gerard said, 'What'll we do?' but there was so much noise he could hardly be heard.

'All I want is a short black,' said Tom, who hadn't actually heard what Gerard had said.

'I think,' said Gina, straining through the thick hubbub of talk, 'that we'll look for somewhere else next week.'

'What did you say?' said Ann.

'Agreed,' said Tom, adjusting his chair in its cramped position, and resigning himself to a long wait for his short black, 'I'm the same: can't hear myself speak.'

Two Hospitals

When she came home from shopping Louise complained of feeling unusually tired and cold. 'Jim', she said, 'I could be coming down with something. I don't want any lunch; I think I'll go straight to bed and see if I can sleep it off.' So after putting the shopping away I got myself a sandwich and cup of tea, and went back to the computer to read the international news. Then I remembered to write an email to an old friend in Wales, which I'd been putting off for over a week now, so by the time I'd run through an outline of our doings over the last month and sent it off it was almost 4 o'clock, and I'd spent more than half the afternoon in the study. And apparently Louise was still asleep. I tiptoed into the bedroom and found her sitting on the edge of the bed hunched over in pain.

'I'm feeling dreadful,' she said, 'how long have I been asleep?'

'Almost three hours. I was getting worried. Where does it hurt?' I sat next to her on the bed and placed a hand lightly on her back.

'Nowhere specific; I'm aching all over…'

'Sounds like it could be 'flu. Have you taken any paracetamol?'

'Actually I think I'm going to be sick… could you get me the bucket from the laundry.'

But when I got back she'd left the bedroom and was standing helplessly beside the *en suite* toilet staring at a wide splash of brownish vomit that had mostly missed the bowl and landed on the tiled floor.

'Sorry…' she muttered, 'It just came so sudden, I was lucky not to do it in the bedroom…'

She sat back on the bed while I cleaned up the mess with toilet paper and then the mop and bucket, noting that what she'd thrown up was recognizable as last night's dinner and this morning's breakfast. Practically nothing had been digested. When I came back from emptying it all into the downstairs toilet she was lying on her side at the foot of the bed and making pitiful little moaning sounds.

'You'd better get back into bed,' I said, and pulled back the covers for her.

'I thought I'd f-feel b-better after bringing it all up, but I d-don't; my stomach is sore, and this p-pain all over my body is if anything w-worse.'

Her voice and lips trembled, and her shoulders shook under the navy dressing gown. She got under the blankets again, and I searched in the bathroom cupboard until I found the thermometer. To my surprise her temperature showed normal.

'Can you bring the bucket,' she said, 'I feel like I'm going to be sick again,' and she stayed sitting up, propped against both our pillows. And she did vomit again but only a small quantity this time, most of it liquid. She stayed like this, sitting up in bed with the bucket under her chin, continuing to spit small eruptions of slimy fluid for the next half hour or so. By six o'clock her shivering had become more violent and her groans of pain almost constant. I was stumped as to the cause. The Covid injection about ten days earlier? Possibly. The clinic would be closed now, so I couldn't ring the doctor. I was still favouring the 'flu idea when the ring tone started up on my mobile ('By the Seaside') and our daughter Molly's voice came through asking about borrowing the trailer to move some household stuff later in the week. I told her about her mother's present state.

'Sounds like gastro,' she said, 'there's practically an epidemic going round Geelong at the moment. Kids are staying home from school in droves.'

'But she doesn't have a temperature.'

'If the vomiting doesn't stop you'd better get her to the hospital,' she said. 'Do you want me to come over and help?'

'No, no, you've got enough to do getting the kids' dinner and all – I can manage.'

Louise suddenly spoke up, 'An ambulance,' she muttered through her shivering, 'don't drive me – get an ambulance; they t-take you straight into emergency without having to w-wait'.

Molly rang off, and I phoned triple zero. The woman who answered took our details, and then insisted that I give Louise some aspirin while we waited for the paramedics to arrive.

'She doesn't like aspirin,' I told her.

'That doesn't matter,' the woman said, 'I need you to give her some aspirin.'

'She's had some paracetamol.'

'It's okay for her to have both sir, so give her some aspirin.'

I turned to Louise, whose face was still distorted with pain, issuing little moaning noises.

'She's telling me to give you aspirin,' I said.

Almost in anger she said, 'I don't take aspirin! Just get me to the hospital!'

'She doesn't take aspirin!' I relayed into the phone, 'we just want the ambulance.'

'They're on their way, sir.' Good, she'd relented. 'I'm going to hang up now,' she continued, 'but just keep her comfortable until they get there. You have a good evening sir.'

'Have a good arsehole', I said to myself. Jesus Christ, who teaches them to say stuff like that? Someone's idea of professional courtesy, of what Americans in sit-coms say in these situations. Fuck good evening.

Within a few minutes the doorbell rang and two blue-uniformed paramedics, a small young woman with a pony tail and an overweight even younger man with a bushy black beard, pressed into the house holding clipboards and equipment, led by me to the bedroom. They took over proceedings; they asked questions, I answered, corrected occasionally by Louise from the bed, who seemed to be intent on showing me to be forgetful and ill-informed, both more-or-less true. The doorbell rang again and another pair of paramedics appeared in the entry, this time an older man, along with a tall young fellow who looked too much like Harrison Ford, and who promptly assumed command. Apparently the two teams were just about to change shift when the call came, so both teams attended.

'Which hospital do you want us to take her to?' the handsome one asked.

I stalled at saying the public hospital, mainly because I wasn't sure of its name any more; things change so often these days. Again Louise piped in, this time from between the first two paramedics, who were supporting her under each arm in the hallway. 'Geelong P-public.'

'You don't have private insurance?' asked the Ford lookalike.

I checked with Louise. 'We do, don't we?'

'I d-dropped it last year,' she replied, 'I told you about it at the t-time.'

I shrugged at the paramedic and said, 'Geelong Public.'

'University Hospital,' said Harrison Ford to his sleepy older colleague.

It was already dark when they placed Louise on the trolley and wheeled her out to the ambulance, a large van-type vehicle with the side door open revealing a brightly lit interior full of gleaming equipment, like some celestial space capsule. At Louise's suggestion I chose not to go with them to the hospital, but would come later in our own car so I could get home either with her or on my own, depending on what happened at the hospital. So I saw the two ambulances off, and scanning the house fronts across the street, guessed the neighbours would be enjoying this rare bit of drama of blue lights flashing and engines running, conversations in the driveway, and whatever intriguing implications it all might have. I gave the invisible watchers a neighbourly wave, and returned to stump up the front steps into the house.

Back inside I made an omelette and a piece of toast, fed and talked to the cat and organised myself for a wait at the hospital – gathered up the novel Louise had been reading, and a book of John McGahern stories for myself, and made sure my phone was charged. It was about seven-thirty by the time I arrived at the emergency department, and immediately I walked in my heart sank; the smallish area was packed with people, either sitting tensely, or bored or asleep, draped over friends in chairs, or sitting on the floor against a wall because there were no seats left. Obviously most of them had been there for hours, waiting for admission. At the far end was a glass wall, behind which were young women conversing with patients through a narrow opening in the glass, which was clearly designed to protect them against any trouble from the public. There were three such openings, each one at the end of a coloured line painted on the floor, each with its purpose spelled out beside the line in the appropriate colour – blue for administration enquiries, yellow for the triage nurse, and red for Covid-19 enquiries. The latter one was not attended, the yellow one had a long queue of people waiting to talk with the nurse, and the blue one had a short queue of people who were being briefly questioned and then directed to join the yellow queue.

I looked around for Louise, but couldn't immediately see her. 'Ah, she's gone in,' I thought, but then I saw with alarm that a wheelchair parked in a dark corner of an ante-room to the main waiting area contained her sleeping or unconscious figure awkwardly tipping sideways from the wheelchair. I hastened to her, and as I straightened her up she woke.

'What's happening?' I asked.

Painfully, she lifted her head. Her face was grey, and she struggled to speak. She was clutching a white plastic vomit bag, its circular mouth held open by a rubber ring. 'They said someone would come and attend to me, but no-one's been; how long have I been here?'

'You came in over an hour ago; hasn't anyone seen you? Interviewed you?'

I joined the administration queue, falling in behind three people, then stood hopping from one foot to the other and rubbing my hands with anger and impatience. After ten or so minutes I got to the woman behind the glass wall, and gave her Louise's details. 'She needs to be seen straight away,' I urged. In a bored, matter-of-fact manner she replied, 'Yes, we know about her, and someone will get to interview her as soon as possible, but we're very busy and a lot of people have come in before her.'

'But she needs urgent attention; didn't the paramedics tell you that?'

'No, the paramedic officer did *not* say it was an urgent case, so I'm afraid she's just going to have to wait until we have a chance to assess her. I'll call her name when we're ready for her, okay?'

'Well how long will that be?'

'I can't tell you that. It won't be sooner than half an hour; we'll call her name when we're ready for her. Please just take a seat.'

I went back to Louise, only to find someone sitting in my seat near her wheelchair. There were no other empty ones left, so I stood beside her and tried to comfort her as best I could. By this time she had resumed groaning, and was clearly growing more distressed by the minute. The woman who'd sat in my chair soon realised the situation, and, spotting a newly vacated chair farther along the room, she quickly moved. So it was now a question of waiting and hoping. God knows what she's got, I thought; it must be gastro. Or food poisoning – the fish last night. But why haven't I got it? And she doesn't have diarrhoea. With no high temperature it doesn't seem like the 'flu; this continual vomiting must mean a tummy bug, but then she is in such a bad way, in such general pain, and looking awful, it feels worse than that.

I tried to read my book, but after six or seven failed attempts to make sense of the same page, I gave up. There was no way Louise could read hers; it was all she could do to handle the pain. Her groans were still coming, and I was getting angrier; unworthy thoughts constantly nagged at me: this shouldn't be happening, it is absurd — look at these people, waiting in mute victimhood, the abject, the social bottom-feeders. We don't belong amongst this crowd, we aren't that poor, we're middle-class, so we should have middle-class medical privileges and protection. What was she thinking, cancelling the insurance? I remembered that a year ago Covid was reducing our self-managed super fund pension so much that we were trying to live on about a third of our usual income. Louise sensibly insisted we reduce expenditure, that we couldn't continue to live as we had. It was even possible we could lose the house, which was still burdened with a mortgage. So we cancelled a number of insurance policies, including the private health. She pointed out that the public hospitals had all the necessary equipment and expertise to deal with serious problems, and all for free — well, virtually. The trouble is, everyone else is thinking the same way, so this overcrowding is the price you pay.

Finally, my patience ran out; I took out my phone, looked up the number of Southern Faith private hospital, and rang them. Yes, a smoothly friendly voice said, their emergency department was open; it will close at midnight. They were not exceptionally busy, so if he brought her in they would see her straight away. I pushed the button to end the call.

'That's it,' I said, 'enough of this; it's going to be hours before they see you here, so I'm taking you over to Southern Faith.' Louise was so bound up in her pain that she hardly registered what I was saying. 'I'll bring the car round to the doorway,' I said and headed off. The car was only a few minutes away, and on my return it was easy enough to drive into the emergency parking area, leave the engine running, dash in and collect her in the wheelchair and get her into the front passenger seat. I carelessly pushed the empty wheelchair along the footpath, where it banged to a halt against the wall. Fuck 'em, they can retrieve it, I said aloud. I wanted a little payback, though I knew they didn't deserve it. Then I drove out into the quiet street. Anger gave way to a hopeful kind of urgency, a feeling that I was at least doing something, rather than just sitting waiting on the patronage of others. But as we drove Louise was making these scrannel noises of distress, as if she were about to break into weird song but tinged with a kind of plea, a little note of despair rounding it off at the end of each cry, and it was driving me to distraction; it reminded me of the persistent importuning squawk young magpies make in the garden every Spring. I wished she could stop it, but of course I would say nothing – I just focussed on taking the slickest route through the dark trafficless streets of the town.

The driveway into the Southern Faith emergency area was clear and there were plenty of spaces near the entrance. I held Louise close while we staggered together like weird competitors in a three-legged race across the black asphalt. We stood before the all-glass entrance for a second or two, wayfarers bereft of the secret password, until with almost cheerful automation a panel suddenly slid open. Inside was a large, warm, comfortably furnished waiting area completely empty of patients. On the right was an office with a window, and a young woman sitting behind it smiled as if she was expecting us. I sat Louise in a chair while I went to the window and gave the woman the personal details she asked for. Then came the demand. 'It will be $230 up front for the emergency room treatment, and if it turns out she needs to stay overnight, that will be $1350 per night. We ask for three nights in advance, but we refund what she doesn't use.'

'So how much do you want now?'

'Just the $230, and hopefully she won't need to stay overnight.'

I handed over my credit card. Jesus, I thought, I could be forking out over four thousand dollars before I leave here tonight. But I couldn't dwell on this, couldn't let expense come into it. All that mattered was that they sorted out the problem and got her well again; to hell with the money. Figures on my computer screen, that's all.

A tall, black-bearded orderly came through the double doors with a wheelchair, carefully helped Louise into it and disappeared back through the doors with her. I presumed it was all right to follow, so I did. No one stopped me (I half expected them to; I always feel like I'm trespassing when I enter expensive-looking interiors).

The emergency area was massive and brilliant; the gleaming floor, ceiling, walls, were bled out to anaemic hues – pale cream, chalky white, chrome silver; rooms with empty beds opened off the main passageway, with adjoining areas cluttered by specialised equipment standing around gurneys, enamelled machines attached to cables, and little red and green lights blinking lonely and dutiful on walls. It was an opulent technologied desert. The temperature was warm enough to shed coats and jackets. The smell was absent. At first there was no-one in sight, but eventually, as required by whatever procedure was to take place next, suitably professional women – they were mostly women – would arrive to take matters in hand. Two nurses in white gowns removed Louise's clothing, put her in a patient's gown and helped her into bed. They hooked her up to a blood pressure monitor, and said the doctor would be along soon. In the meantime, I sat in the chair beside her bed and reached for her hand, protruding spotted and vulnerable from the white sheet; the hand was cold, trembling. And though she had ceased the groaning sounds, she was still closed-in on herself, looking down with unseeing eyes, out of touch with everything around her in an effort to brace against the pain. Already her personhood was lost in the patient category.

I opened my book and tried to read. Again it was useless; my mind was in chaos. I looked around. The contrast between this place and the public hospital was marked, mostly by its absence of patients; there was only the staff. And yet not fifteen minutes away that other place was crowded with suffering bodies, hopefuls waiting for hours to see a doctor, like inhabitants of a Third World country. Madness. I passed the silence trying to identify the equipment in the room, hoping that it might bring order to my mind: a mobile drip stand with a transparent bag of fluid and tube hung over a hook; various complicated machines on wheels stood unconnected, their monitors dead; a white enamelled robotic-looking piece displaying its name below the black monitor: 'Acme Haematology Analyser' – American, like its Roadrunner brandname. Over against the far wall a trolley bearing a clutter of suture trays, bowls, packets of sterile swabs and towels waited to be called upon. Propped in the corner beside the trolley was a pair of wooden crutches, which might or might not have been recently discarded by a patient. *Take up thy bed and walk*, came into my head from somewhere. Behind me, patterning the wall above the bed, was a gallery of plaques giving advice and warnings 'Do Not Switch Off', 'Non-Suction', 'Alarm', 'Emergency use only', and amongst them a cluttered array of knobs, switches, power points (red, for some reason), dials, attachments, mysterious instruments hanging in wall supports, their black or white coiled cables dangling, and a whiteboard attached to the wall already showing my wife's name as the patient, and a nurse Crowley and Doctor Helger in attendance, scrawled in black marker pen; yet another of the current generation with child's handwriting, I noted; because of the peculiar way they grip the pen? These riches were hospital culture at its most bountiful, and I was selfish enough at this moment to be glad of it. Yet I remained tense and fearful about what might yet unfold in the next hours, and hating that any of this should happen at all. I was tired but jumpy, my nerves frayed at the edges, and I wished I could relax enough to get some sleep. But that was not likely.

A young doctor entered the room, her brisk footsteps clattering. She took Louise through a series of questions about her symptoms, while a nurse was putting a temperature gauge into her ear. 'We need to check for infection, so let's do a blood analysis,' she said to the nurse, and then to me she said 'You're welcome to stay while we're doing tests, and we'll discuss the results when they come through, which could be an hour or so.' Meanwhile the two nurses fussed around again making Louise comfortable, gave her some tablets for the pain, and then departed, leaving us alone among the gadgets and in the fluorescent glare flooding the whole emergency area, humming with a low, constant white noise.

We talked spasmodically, until the painkiller kicked in and Louise was able to put her head back onto the pillow and close her eyes, dozing I hoped. Again the difference between the hospitals sprang to mind. Louise had told me a year ago that Southern Faith, this very place, had initially been planned as a second *public* hospital for the region, but that a political decision had been made to hand it to the private sector. I took out my phone and looked it up. Information on the political aspect of the change did not appear on the search. All I could find were Southern Faith's own website and blogs, noting that it called itself a 'not-for-profit' organisation with religious connections, owning sites in several locations around Victoria. I took 'not-for-profit' to mean entitlement to tax concessions. If they don't make a profit from what they're charging, there must be something wrong; I guess eye-watering specialists' fees don't come under 'profit'. My state of helpless fear and anger was growing more general. It wasn't just the money, but the disparity; it is everywhere, and getting worse. The power itself – the power to materialise self-interest – is maybe rarer, concentrated in the hands of fewer and fewer, but the practise of converting that power into assets is growing more common, in all senses – more blatant, more greedy, more indecent. But it seems there is no stopping it.

Such thoughts get you nowhere, and were certainly not helping me cope with the immediate situation. Forcing myself back to my book, I managed at last, with the aid of McGahern's narrative gifts, to slide into a different, imagined world: yet another bitter story around Moran, the author's proxy for his domineering policeman father; how fruitfully that man had dictated so much of McGahern's way of feeling. Again and again he came back to it, mining the rich vein of memories, spinning new scenes of disappointment, of failure, of unforgiving bonds, and the magical way the minutiae of humble lives contrive to suggest the past and present of Ireland herself.

The doctor, followed by a nurse, came back in and said, 'There's no infection according to the blood test. So what I'll do now is send her off for an x-ray, and maybe we'll do a CT scan as well. How are you feeling now?'

Louise opened her eyes. So she hadn't been in a proper sleep, anyway. 'The pain is still there,' she croaked. 'I keep thinking I'm going to throw up again, but there isn't anything to come up… uh-oh,' And just as she said this she lurched forward and quickly brought the vomit bag, which had been clutched in her left hand all this time, up to her mouth; a retch followed by wind issued, and she spat into the bag the little that came. The doctor stood alongside and touched Louise's shoulder with a consoling hand. 'I'll go and order the x-ray now,' she said, 'I think we'd better do a CT scan as well…' She left the room.

The bearded young man who had wheeled her in earlier came in and, easing the brakes off the wheels, guided the bed with Louise on it out through the wide doorway, followed by the doctor and nurses; I was left sitting by myself in the empty room. By the clock on the opposite wall it was coming up to eleven-thirty. Again the building was quiet enough to hear the bland hum. I tried to get back to McGahern, but having finished the story I'd been reading, I didn't feel like making the effort of starting a new one, so I put the book back into my bag and decided to take a stroll around the emergency area.

Walking about, I was affected once again by the fear, the apprehension of the intruder into forbidden territory, and felt that any moment an orderly or whoever would appear and tell me I was trespassing, and to go back to my chair and wait patiently until my legitimate grounds of concern, that is my wife, returned. I tried to make my footfalls quieter, as I roamed the broad corridors, taking in the glossy splendour of it all. Suddenly my worst fear materialised: a nurse emerged from a room up ahead and was coming my way. I'll say I'm looking for a toilet, I decided, as the distance between us closed. But as she got near the nurse simply smiled and said, 'Hi,' and walked on past. Relief. In fact, if I thought about it, no-one has ever told me I don't belong anywhere; it's just the way certain places make me feel.

Back in the room, I began another of the Irishman's stories, but had not got to the second page when Louise was wheeled back in by the young, bearded man, who positioned and braked her bed. She was lying on her back, but was awake. 'How was it?' I asked. She shrugged, as if to say 'It was an x-ray – nothing to say about it.' But then she did say, 'The doctor is organising a CT scan.'

It was another half hour before someone came to take her off again, and I was surprised to see it was a different young man taking her this time. Indian looking, no beard. Same routine, and I was set for another wait, trying again to read, when, after only about fifteen minutes the doctor entered the room alone. Standing before me, continually lifting the toe of her brown medium-heeled right shoe, occasionally with her finger dragging a lock of her blonde hair away from her face, she spoke her thoughts: by a process of elimination she was ruling out an infection – no high temperature, nothing abnormal showing in the blood count, no diarrhoea. The x-ray was inconclusive, but something was showing in her small intestine, picked up by the CT scan. She thought it probable that Louise had a bowel blockage, but she was waiting to consult with a radiologist. 'Meanwhile,' she said, 'let's get a tube in there to relieve some of the pressure.'

A few minutes later the smaller nurse came back in, and together they put a drip feed of saline into Louise's arm, and then carefully inserted a tube through her nostril and fed it down and down. 'How is that? Are you ok with it?' the nurse said, continuing to feed it through, and Louise replied, 'A bit uncomfortable, but it's okay.' Within a minute or so the semi-transparent bag began to fill with brownish liquid. 'Ah, there we go,' said the doctor, 'that should help things a bit.' Louise let out a weak laugh. 'Oh yes', she said, 'I see what that is.' It was not just what lay in her stomach that was flowing into the bag – it was part of the contents of her bowel. It was shit. And, unnaturally, it was coming upwards.

The doctor went away again, and by the time she returned it was getting on for one-forty-five. Where had the time gone? The hours had been chewed up in a sequence of activities punctuating deadening stretches of boredom. How much longer was this going to go on?

Sitting on the bed, addressing Louise, the doctor summarised the situation. 'Okay,' she said, 'here's what I think: I'm pretty sure you have an obstructed bowel – on the scan I can see something in there that looks like a blockage, maybe caused by a twist or adhesions. It could possibly be cleared by use of an oral agent – a gel maybe – or it might clear itself in time. They often do. But it's also possible that it will need surgery to clear it. So this all means that you need to be admitted and a bed found, and frankly we don't want to do that here. You don't have private insurance, and the cost would be huge.' The thought flashed through my mind – they're concerned they won't get their money. She turned to me, 'So here's what we can do: we've contacted Geelong University Hospital – the public hospital – and asked about a bed. They don't have one at the moment, but our surgeon will contact the surgery registrar there and see what can be done. It is really better that they take her in. I'll give you a letter to take to GUH, referring you to the surgery registrar and explaining the situation.'

My heart sank. I was so tired now, just wanted to go home and crawl into bed. I'd been prepared for none of what had happened in the past seven or so hours, and my emotions – about the waiting, about the money, and most of all about Louise's condition – were in a jangled mess. Maybe I could just leave them to it – they would likely take her in an ambulance over to GUH when they had a bed free – and meanwhile they would keep her here monitoring her situation. I said to the doctor, 'Can you arrange an ambulance to take her to GUH?'

'I don't think that's a good idea,' she said, 'we have no idea how long it might take for it to come – it could be five minutes, or not come till the morning. It would be best if you take her and wait with her until they find a bed for her. We've done all we can here, but take your time, get your things together, and we'll help you get your wife out to the car.'

Again my anger rose, again mixed with the debilitating weariness. The thought of going back to the public hospital, of going through it all again – the waiting, the bodies strewn about. It was the run-around once again; I felt I'd been conned. Sure, they'd kept her comfortable, had formed a diagnosis. But for $230. And it's the money that takes priority, not curing the patient. Maybe they didn't have the expertise on hand, but whatever the reason they were not prepared to put Louise first. It was all too much, and I wanted either to cry or scream at the top of my lungs. But of course I did neither. What I did do, the only defiance I could muster, was to reject their offers of help, apart from placing her back in the wheelchair. 'No, no,' I said tensely, 'I don't need you to come out to the car; just leave it to me, thank you, I'll manage.'

I wheeled Louise out through the sliding exit door, and immediately the night wind slapped my face. As we made our way across the car park the air bit into my lungs, and I had a coughing fit trying to get her into the passenger seat of the car. At least she had stopped moaning with pain, now that the pressure in her gut had eased. But she was still weak and fragile. Fifteen minutes later I walked her into the GUH emergency waiting room once again, and settled her into a chair. There were not as many people waiting now – maybe twenty – and only a few standing in the two queues. Clutching the buff envelope containing the letter from Southern Faith I once again joined the blue line queue, which was being forwarded to the yellow line after a brief interview; the window for the red line, the Covid queue, was completely closed. Within a minute or two I reached the woman at the window and held out the envelope to her, which she did not take.

'I was here before,' I began to explain, 'but my wife…'

'Name.'

I told her, and again tried to pass the letter to her. 'This letter from Southern Faith to the registrar explains our situation, and…'

'There's nothing I can do; you have to join the queue to see the triage nurse,' she said firmly, still not accepting the letter. She was not going to listen to anything I had to say that might challenge established routine. I gave up and moved over to the yellow line, behind three others. At the window a young mother with a baby was engaged in a long, chatty conversation with the nurse, who seemed no older than the mother, and in no hurry to deal with whatever she'd come about. For a good five minutes they chatted, broke into occasional guffaws, and then the nurse reached out and took the baby's temperature with a hand-held thermometer. Still they talked.

I was ready to scream at the nurse, at the administration officer, at the emergency department, at the whole bloody hospital and its pathetically inadequate, careless, bankrupt system. When would they realise that Louise needed immediate attention? Didn't they know she could *die*?

The young woman with the baby left the window and sat down. In front of me the short broad woman with grey hair stepped up to the window and talked in muffled tones while the nurse consulted her computer. She responded to a series of questions, then the nurse left her post and disappeared into an adjoining room at the back. We waited. The broad woman turned her head round and smiled apologetically at me, showing a mouth with several front teeth missing. 'Sorry,' she said in a foreign accent. I was too impatient to reply, just nodded and looked down. I turned to see if Louise was okay; she had her eyes closed and head back uncomfortably, sliding forward in the chair. The triage nurse returned and addressed the woman. 'He'll be out soon, if you'll just take a seat. Won't be long,' and the woman complied.

I stepped up and, as before, moved to hand the envelope through the opening in the window; the nurse took it. 'What's this?' she said.

'I've come from Southern Faith. This is a letter to the registrar about my wife – they've apparently spoken to the surgeon here, who knows it's urgent and has agreed to see her straight away…'

She opened the envelope and read the letter. She then consulted her computer, and while doing so said, 'We can't admit her straight away – we don't have a bed for her right now. What did they tell you at Southern Faith?'

'Just that they couldn't do the procedure there because we don't have private insurance, and that they had spoken to someone here who said they'd be able to admit her when a bed was available, which they said would be very soon…'

The nurse produced a short, sharp exhalation. It was a sound no longer than a split second, but it had a kind of shape, told a little story, beginning in a spirit of brutal derision at what I'd just said. This was followed by a tone of weariness, brought on by the demands, abusive comments, humiliations, or simply deserving pleas (they were the hardest) made on her patience throughout the long day. Then self-consciousness turned it into a hint – just a hint – of regret, and a self-admonition to shut up. But too late – it was out, a scoffing 'Hah!

The effect was to produce an icy fury in me. Calm and steady, I looked directly into her face and almost whispered, 'Oh, you thought that was a joke, did you?'

She paused while a whirl of thoughts flashed through her head, and then a survival instinct kicked in, and she broke. Enacting the realization of impending disaster, she put her fingers up to her hair and said, 'Oh, I'm terribly sorry, no, no I don't think it was a joke. Please, I do apologize sir, that was unforgivable...'

After a long pause in which she returned my direct gaze, she turned back to the task in hand, to her computer, folding up the letter and returning it to the envelope, handing it back and making sympathetic sounds about getting someone to assess Louise as quickly as possible. She even indulged in a little friendly chat. 'You realize,' she said, 'that Southern Faith was meant to be ours? It was meant to be Geelong's second public hospital, until the government changed its mind and made it private. Outrageous.'

'I know', I said, 'I know.'

'So would you excuse me for a moment Mr Conlan, and I'll see what's happening in the ward.' She went out through the door at the rear of the room again. I went back to Louise; she hadn't moved in the chair, and seemed to be still asleep. After three or four minutes, the nurse returned.

'If you'd like to bring your wife up and sit over there near the double doors, we're hoping to find you a bed shortly.'

'Thank you.'

I went back to Louise and woke her, got her up out of the chair, and together like wounded soldiers we shuffled and staggered across the room to the new position, a row of five seats within three metres of the double doors to the emergency ward. I'd noticed this row earlier, correctly concluding it was a waiting area for patients due for imminent admission. We sat down to wait, but did so now in a mood of rising hope. I made sure the strap of her handbag was securely strung around her neck, then took my book out of my shoulder bag, and settled. This new outlook enabled me to actually make sense of the opening paragraphs of the story I'd been trying to read since around midnight.

I got no further, however, because a young male orderly broke through the double doors with a wheelchair, quickly hoisted Louise into it and took her back through the double doors. I was left to gather up my things and follow them, but already they had turned out of the short corridor and were out of sight. I wandered in, and for some minutes looked about for her; the corridor opened into a cramped maze of cubicles, passageways, trolleys and gurneys, with nurses, orderlies, doctors, office assistants all busy trying to keep out of each other's way in the crowded area. A nurse must have noticed the anxious look on my face, because she quickly pointed along a narrow corridor to a line of cubicles. And there at last I found her, already lying on a bed, awake and talking with a doctor. It was in hand now, I could see, Louise was already more relaxed, and the doctor, a handsome young fellow, with a foreign name on his ID tag but no sign of an accent, explained to us both that he would be monitoring her situation through the night and would perform whatever procedures were necessary to resolve the problem.

'Call in the morning,' he said, 'and we'll bring you up to date on her progress.'

I felt myself loosen inside, as if an internal tie had come

undone. That was it then, the worst was over, I could walk away from it at last. Somehow the system had finally delivered, despite the chaos, the indifference to individual feelings; she would be safe here. I leaned over and kissed her on the mouth. 'I'll get off home now, and call in the morning.'

'Yes love, you go home, get some sleep; you must be tired. I'll be fine now – they'll look after me,' and she threw a look at the doctor standing at the end of the bed, 'you'll look after me, won't you Rahul?' It slightly surprised me that she already knew his first name; but then, she was always good at that kind of thing – taking in immediate facts, times, dates, names, especially of handsome young men. The slightly flirty girl had never been quite outgrown.

Driving home through the deserted streets certain nagging thoughts wouldn't quite leave me: for all that relief of being admitted, she still has a blocked bowel; the cause still has to be properly identified, treated, and surgery might still be necessary, and therein lay potential danger. I recalled a friend years ago, involving bowel cancer, and for all their medical confidence, they couldn't save him. With an effort I pulled myself out of this line of thought; I was too tired, and the relief too welcome, to keep on. Forget it – get home, get into bed.

When I let myself in the front door, Millie the cat was there to greet me, sitting in her little statuesque manner in the middle of the foyer looking her tabby-and-white best. She meowed and followed me down to the kitchen. It was after four o'clock in the morning, but I wasn't quite ready for bed. I needed to allow the tiredness to take over, drive out the tension of thinking. I made a hot chocolate drink and a slice of toast and vegemite, turned on the television, brought up a recorded episode of *QI*, and munched and drank, watching the witticisms fly. Millie climbed purring onto my lap, and stayed there until the program was over, and weariness got the better of me, and I realised I'd finally reached the point when I might be able to fall asleep. Any moment soon I would make the move to bed; no doubt Millie would be happy to keep me company.

A Higher Learning

Andrew pressed the gate bell – a strangely domestic device for a prison – and waited feeling important and, he permitted himself the vanity, moderately brave. A small door in the gate opened and a thin-lipped guard said, 'Yeah?'

'Andrew Elliot.'

The guard's eyes remained motionless, like a doll's.

'I've come to take the, ah, literature class at four-thirty.'

'Education are we. Who sent ya?'

'It's all supposed to have been arranged between the Adult Education Centre and the governor. I'm a bit early, I know, but I was hoping to have a preliminary discussion with the students about the form of the syllabus first.'

'Wait there,' said the guard, and slammed the door. Time passed. The gate was rotting and not so impregnable as it looked from a distance. Not so romantic. Andrew began to feel affronted. This was not the welcome he was expecting; after all, he had gone to some trouble preparing for this new teaching venture for the Centre, taking on part-time classes at the Oxford Prison to augment his modest postgraduate scholarship allowance. He'd sketched out exciting and appropriate lessons: *Individualism and Society*; *The Literature of Existential Revolt*. Also, he had bought himself a new corduroy jacket and, a new colour for him, a dark brown shirt. Surely they realise that the educational welfare of prisoners is a very serious matter. Still he waited; the wind was getting cooler, and kept blowing his hair the wrong way across his forehead; his discomfort was becoming intolerable. He pressed the bell again, holding his finger down considerably longer. The face reappeared.

'Yeah?'

'I thought you must have forgotten me. It's almost twenty past, and I have to start at half-past.'

'Come in then,' said the guard, and led him through a paved, deserted courtyard into a small hut. 'Wait in the waiting room,' he said, and departed.

The tiny room stank of old cigarette butts and was littered with yellow plastic chairs, one of which bore a woman in black gazing through a window into the courtyard. She smoked a cigarette and ignored Andrew; probably the *de facto* of one of the inmates, he presumed. Eventually the guard returned and said the Governor wanted to see him.

'But my class…' he protested.

'They won't go far away,' the guard chuckled.

The governor's offices were plush, rubber-treed and furnished with young females, one of whom escorted him to an enormous room where a greyer David Niven smiled out from behind a desk. It was some minutes before Andrew noticed that one of his arms – the right – was artificial, the pink plastic hand shelved on the desk in front of him. But he forced himself to ignore this and instead try to concentrate on a rather long speech the governor was making whilst pouring two sherries with his good hand. By the time Andrew grasped the sense of the speech it was just concluding '… I have always been a Great Believer in education, especially for those prisoners who would not be staying for a long period.'

Andrew wondered for a moment if there wasn't something odd about that statement, but he was cut off by the Governor's question 'And what do you propose to teach the men?'

'I thought basically I would concentrate on the "outsider" theme, you know the notion that social rebellion can be action on a higher moral plane, or at least more authentic, than the comfortable, hypocritical role-playing in which conventional societal man submerges himself. We would read novels, plays, elementary sociology. Would you like to see my proposed syllabus in detail?'

'Er, no, no thank you,' said the Governor, 'I'll take your word for it. Sounds fascinating. You may find some difficulty in getting them to concentrate, but don't let that beat you. You are an Australian I take it? I should imagine talking to convicts will come second nature to you, eh? What?' and the conspiratorial laugh that came with this was meant to ensure that Andrew took the joke in the right spirit. Which, under the circumstances, he did, and laughed weakly in response. Suddenly the governor rose to signify the end of the interview, and Andrew had to swallow three fingers of sherry in one gulp, which brought tears to his eyes. 'Let me offer you a word of advice, if I may,' said the governor benevolently. 'You'll find that a few of them are obsessed by what they will call "their case", and will try to get you caught up in some kind of appeal or petition or other on their behalf. If that happens, take no notice and get them back to the point. Another thing is that many of them are besotted with sex, and will want you to talk about it *ad nauseam*; for obvious humane reasons I should discourage that, too. Steer clear of those two areas and I'm sure you'll win their respect and have some very enjoyable classes. Good luck, and you know what to do if there's anything you want.'

What a charming and helpful man, thought Andrew, and reached forward eagerly to shake hands, only to feel with horror that he had snatched up the plastic replica. Thinking it best to continue as if everything were normal, rather than release his hold, Andrew held on tight and pumped the limb vigorously, while the governor looked alarmed. After a brief struggle the prosthesis was finally tugged free, and the two men parted under a murky cloud of silence.

The guard led him to an ancient building with tiny barred windows and a great steel door. They waited while two locks were opened and the door slid back. When it clanged shut behind him Andrew had a spasm of fear, then pleasure: that's what a prisoner must feel the first time, he thought. Only gradually did shapes emerge from the dim interior – staircases like scaffolding, skeletal tables, chairs, walls, cages. Shadowy figures played table-tennis as through a thin fog, the 'pok' from their blows echoing loudly, their voices thunderous. All shades were a variety of grey – the metal, the concrete, the clothing, the stone, the weak light from the windows, the gaseous brilliance from the strip lights. There was a constant warm stink as if a rubbish bin had overturned. They went upstairs to a tiny green room noisy with men propped against walls and perched on steel tables. The guard shouted over the noise, 'Here y'are. Teacher of the literature class: answer your names.' Andrew's mouth went dry and his mind panicky as the names were read out. The room stank of bodies. 'They're all yours till five-thirty,' said the guard, and checked his watch, 'which gives you about ten minutes today.' The metal door slammed behind him, and was locked. More as a gesture of appeasement than authority, Andrew held up an open right hand. The noise continued unchecked.

'Shuddup!' said a voice, and the noise died. The man was not only blond-haired, but his eyebrows and lashes were colourless and his skin bleached, which along with his weepy, red-rimmed eyes made him seem weak. His face, nose and shoulders were narrow, and his authority over the other men would have been surprising if it had not been for an extraordinary mouth, which appeared to have been inserted into his face at a forty-five degree angle, moving continually and cleverly, irrepressibly truculent, severe and dangerous.

Andrew apologized for being late, and explained to them what he had in mind for the classes, which would begin next week. He asked if there were any particular preferences for books. Someone whispered, 'Christ, we gotta read books'. He waited for a sign of life in their glazed eyes. Eventually, a man with buck teeth, dirty glasses and one-third of an extravagantly mutilated nose said, 'Have you ever read *Never Love a Call Girl* by…'

The blond interrupted, 'You dickhead, Artie, he doesn't mean them sort of books. He mean books that make you think.'

'Think what?' said Artie.

The blond pushed himself off the table and sauntered up to Andrew. 'I'm Stearns,' he said, 'Joseph Kelvin Stearns, but my friends call me Joe. The last teacher was gunna show us some pictures. That's what we like. Good pictures, in colour.'

So keen was Andrew to please that he blurted out, 'What a good idea; I know what we can do – we'll see a film one week and study the same book the following week…' There was some sign of interest at this, though not enough to warrant the degree of Andrew's self-congratulation. I'm coping very nicely, he said to himself as he left the building, 'and tomorrow I must arrange about the films.'

The next week Andrew had his second encounter with the class in the green dungeon. This time the guard did not lock the door, which bolstered his confidence further. He raised his voice above their noise: 'You'll be pleased to know that I've arranged with the governor that we can see a film every fortnight; it will be set up for us in the Chapel, so there should be no problems. Nest week we will start with the film of *Women in Love* by D.H.Lawrence.' There were a couple of whoops for joy. Stearns gave him a flamboyant wink, came up, ruffled his hair and said, 'You're a bewdy, teach.'

Warming to his task now, Andrew announced, 'Now for today I thought we'd have a go at a play reading. Have any of you read *Mathry Beacon* by Giles Cooper? From his bag he produced several copies, which he'd found in the library of the Adult Education Centre, and placed them on the table. They were picked up, flicked through, and carelessly tossed back. Andrew then began to allocate roles, but nobody wanted to play the women's parts.

'We should have Cedric here,' said one.

'Yeah. It's a shame about Cedric,' said Stearns, 'but he's not looking his prettiest right now.' Knowing laughter.

'Did you hear about Cedric?' continued Stearns, 'He had a terrible accident in the tea-queue – someone spilt tea all over his face and he had to go to hospital. An awful shame.' More laughter. Andrew glared.

'Why did you do that?'

'Cause,' said Artie, 'he's in for playin' around with little boys. He's a fucken criminal.'

'Well, isn't that what you are?'

Artie's disfigured face crumpled in deep offence. 'No, I'm not. I'm not guilty. I was set up. I was goin' to talk to you about that…'

'Leave it, leave it,' said Stearns, 'take no notice of him. Walks into a pub and starts floggin' off dud fives, and then he says he was set up.' The others thought this was funny, so Artie laughed too. Stearns went on, 'We don't tolerate queers in here y'know. After all, it's not right is it? I mean, how would you like it teach, if your little boy was got at by one of those maniac bastards. What I'd do, I'd shoot the lot of 'em.'

Andrew tried to protest, but Stearns silenced him with a wave. 'Come on,' he said, 'let's read the bloody play. Artie, you can be one of the women. I'll be one as well.'

This was not quite the atmosphere that Andrew wanted, but he nevertheless signalled the first reader, a thin youth with a skinhead and earrings, to commence. There was a long silence. The youth put his head down close to the book and frowned, his lips pursed tight as if trying to *prevent* sound from escaping. Eventually, some sound broke through: 'Wh… wh… what… a… G… God… for… for…'

Only gradually did Andrew realize what was wrong, and when he did he felt completely ashamed for the youth. The agony continued, '… for… saken end of… the… world to… send… people to', until someone burst out, 'Hey teach, Kneebone can't even read!' The skinhead flung the book down onto the floor and sat back sulkily with his eyes looking nowhere. 'Fuck off,' he muttered.

'Give it to me, give it to me,' said someone else.

'Okay,' said Andrew quickly, 'you start.' This man hesitated also, and then began in similar fashion: 'Wh… wh… wh…' he parodied, and spluttered into laughter, followed by the others. From then on everyone who read did so in mock stammers, punctuated by idiotic laughter, until the whole scheme had disintegrated into shrieks.

Andrew looked down in despair. 'Animals,' he said to himself, 'animals in a zoo.' He didn't know whether to shout at them or run from the cell, though instead of doing either he simply stood hoping for the noise to die down. Finally, Stearns came up. 'Trouble is,' he said, 'they don't like plays. They're all too thick. Besides, they won't cooperate because you see they're resentful of being in here at all. But you take me for instance. I don't mind it too much because this is my fourth stretch and I'm used to it and know how to take it. And when I go outside I've got to get a job and support my wife and kids and that's not much fun. So a little rest in here now and then doesn't worry me, know what I mean?'

Andrew thought to himself, 'I wonder if that relentless glottal stopping is hard to do? It sounds like an affectation, but maybe he can't help it'. Then he thought, 'I am hot. I feel sweaty. I don't trust him.'

'But a lot of these blokes,' Stearns was going on, 'they just can't adjust to the life. They don't like playing along with all these education and rehabilitation and welfare games.'

'Why are you in here this time, then?' said Andrew. Stearns flung an arm towards the far corner of the room, where a sad-faced beanpole of a man languished in silence. 'Hey Terry,' called Stearns, 'teach wants to know how we got lumbered. Shall I tell him?'

Terry grinned and bit the end off a Mars bar. Stearns moved to the front of the room as if about to perform a song, and narrated slickly: 'Terry and me were drivin' along down near Folkestone, and it was such a lovely day that we felt like doin' something interesting, and then we see this feller on a bike. So Terry says let's go and have a word with 'im. We get out of the car – it was on a bridge over a river – and as he rode up to us we could see he was wearin' some sort of cap and had onions – no garlic it was – on his handlebars, so we pulled him off the bike. Terry says to 'im "Where ya goin?", and this feller – he was an old feller – just shrugged and mumbled somethin' we couldn't understand.'

The room was quiet, under the spell of that crafty mouth.

'So Terry says, "empty your pockets" and the old man just shrugged again. Then Terry says, "I don' like garlic; it makes ya bref stink."' A sprinkle of laughter in the room. 'Then I says to the guy – didn't I Terry? – I said, "Don't tell me: your *French*!"'

Everyone except Andrew laughed this time. 'So we got 'im,' concluded Stearns, 'and the bike, and the garlic, and threw 'em all over the bridge and into the river. Unfortunately somebody saw us and told the police.' Stearns finished the story with a slight bow, and drew a round of applause from the audience.

Andrew fought down his indignation, but he was nevertheless determined to knock Stearns down a peg or two. 'And you know what happens now?' he said. Stearns put his head on one side and waited. 'The police will lock you up for every little thing you do wrong from now on, for the rest of your life.'

Continuing to look straight at Andrew, Stearns raised himself backwards onto the table. 'Oh no,' he said with immense seriousness, 'no – I told the governor and I'm telling you: I'm going straight now – I've learned my lesson. I'm never coming back here – straight as a die from now on.'

The room waited for Andrew's reply. He hesitated for a moment, then said, 'Well, we'll have the film next week. That'll do for today.' Then quickly and averting his gaze from making contact with anyone else's, he stuffed his books into his briefcase and slipped out of the room.

Andrew had convinced himself over the course of the following week that the film would be the clincher of his popularity with the class. Certainly *Women in Love* might pass several feet over their nit-ridden heads, he told himself, but all the same they would appreciate my efforts to brighten up their lives. He arrived several minutes early this week, just to ensure that things went smoothly.

'No, no,' he told the guard, who was leading him to the usual cell, 'we'll be in the Chapel this week viewing a film.'

'Ah yes,' said the guards, 'I nearly forgot. The governor sent word to tell you there's been a hitch over the film. He's very sorry, but you'll have to put it off until next week.'

Andrew could feel an attack of asthma coming on – the first for some years. 'Next week? But the class will be expecting it – I promised them. They'll be very disappointed in me.'

After a few moments thought the guard said, 'Well, I don't think you'll find they're too upset about it, and anyway you can make them another promise for next week.'

Inside the cell Andrew stood before the class greeted by pointed silence. His knees felt shaky and his asthma was getting worse. Stearns said, 'Guess what. Very unexpected news. No film.'

Between gasps Andrew apologized, 'There must have been…. some reason… take too long… straighten out… look into it… see to it… film ready for next… week without fail.'

'Oh dear,' said Stearns, 'poor teach isn't well; Artie, get up and give the man a seat.'

Artie's ministrations went beyond the immediate call of duty as he fussed over Andrew's shirt buttons, loosening his collar and tie, and fanning him with a putrid white handkerchief. Andrew was experiencing an old familiar nightmare of himself running up a down escalator pursued by a blind giant, and was telling himself 'I must get them to see it was not my doing… that I'm as disappointed about the film as they are…'

These preoccupations prevented Andrew from noticing that Stearns had quietly slipped from the cell by way of the unlocked door. But he was very aware of the loud complaints of the others, 'like whining schoolboys,' he said to himself.

'I was looking forward to a colour pitcher,' said one. 'There's a good bit of tit in that film,' said another. 'It's all about lesbians,' confided someone else.

Artie sat on the table next to him. 'Look teach. There's something you could do for me when you see the governor. Y'see a feller in the pub gave me that stuff to pass round. I never knew a thing about it… if you tell the governor you believe he'll probably review my case…'

Then Terry was towering, Pisa-like over him and stuffing his mouth with the last wedge of an egg sandwich. 'If you could just slip it in your bag you could bring in some shit for us… but get good stuff. I can pay for it…'

Books, thought Andrew, books, I must get them to talk about books. He straightened up, still fighting for breath, and cried 'Stop! Quiet. Now listen…' This unexpected assertion of authority seemed to work, for the talking stopped. 'What we will now do is discuss the story of *Women*–' But Stearns had stepped into the room with a guard, who said, 'Stearns says you're not well. What's the trouble?'

'Oh, it's nothing… a slight attack of asthma, but I–'

'Slight!' said Stearns. 'His face was blue. He couldn't talk. It's the small room, he can't catch his breath in this sardine tin.' As Andrew looked across at Stearns he was shot a lightning wink, and responded immediately. 'Yes, it's a bit cramped and stuffy in here.'

'He can't hold a proper class in here,' Stearns told the guard, 'Not if he can't breathe. He needs somewhere where there's plenty of room, fresh air.'

The guard looked doubtful. Andrew, almost without thinking, and certainly without at all knowing why, cooperated further by

resuming his gasps and, by straining his solar plexus, causing his face
to colour an alarming mauve.

'The Chapel!' said Stearns, 'that's the best place. We could
have the class in the Chapel.'

The guard still looked uncertain while everyone waited in
silence for his verdict, until finally he could bear the burden no
longer, and agreed to the move. Rattling his keys loudly, the guard
led the prisoners along the promenade, with Stearns comrading it
side by side with a confused Andrew at the rear. He wondered why
Stearns was going to so much trouble to ensure the success of the
lesson.

Although it was part of the cell block, inside it was just like
any other Chapel: a high ceiling, an altar, brassware, marble, a pulpit
and a lectern. It was lit by an amber glow through two stained glass
windows on each side, and there were rows of pews, most with
initials carved in them, and some cushions and hymn books strewn
about. Andrew's spirit rose immediately.

The guard ushered them into the Chapel, left and closed the
door. Stearns waited until he was well away, then shot the bolt
locking them all in. The men lounged into the pews, threw a few
cushions at each other, or rubbed their hands eagerly. Andrew,
feeling it was time he resumed control, went to the front and casually
seated himself on the communion rail. 'This is more like it,' he said,
'now we can get down to some decent discussion in the time we have
left. Perhaps if I begin by outlining some of Lawrence's ideas in the
book…'

'Siddown,' said someone.

'What's the time?' someone asked.

'We've only missed ten minutes,' another said.

'Sit down. Get out of the way,' said more voices, directly at
Andrew. He was confused. He looked about for Stearns, who had
already leaped the communion rail and disappeared behind the altar.

To the accompaniment of smoothly rumbling castors, Stearns backed out from behind the altar pulling a chrome trolley, upon which was a grey-bodied, blank-screened, large television set. He wheeled it round to the front till it was standing before, and partly obscuring, the pulpit. Having obtained general assent to the positioning, Stearns plugged in the long lead and switched it on. 'Channel Four!' they cried in unison. It was switched over. Utter silence. A buzz. Distant music, growing louder, then images of bodies, brief-skirted, long-legged females grinding happily to a rock beat and black harmonies. 'Pan's People,' said Stearns in a voice hoarse with desire, putting his feet up, and followed by several others as they all sat hypnotized, taking in every moment with hungry eyes. Not a word did they say, not a shuffle, nor a cough, nor a laugh, nor any further sign that they were together in a group; each man was intent on his own private paradise, his own vision of perfect freedom.

'Top of the Pops!' said Andrew with disgust.

'Yeah, great,' said Terry, producing a 'Teddy Bear' biscuit from his pocket, and savagely biting off the head. Andrew slunk to the rear of the Chapel and threw himself into the back row. 'Let them stay down in the shit,' he said to himself, 'I've tried to help them, but they're hopeless…'

At a gap in the items Stearns turned round. 'Hey, Teach,' he said, 'come and sit up here next to me. You can't see too well from back there.'

His self-pity became anger. He threw Stearns a look of cold hatred, and with tears of malice in his eyes he thrust into his bag and snatched out his copy of *Women in Love*, which he pretended to read for the rest of the period.

No film ever did turn up. Not the following week, nor the week after, nor the week after that. He gave up apologizing to the class; nobody seemed concerned about it, least of all the men, who seemed never to have believed in the existence of the films anyway. And so every week Stearns got Andrew to persuade the guard to let them in the Chapel, and so every week the literature class consisted of sixty minutes of Top of the Pops, through which Andrew sat tortured with guilt. After the second time, he enquired at the governor's office on his way out, but he was told the governor was not in. He rang twice the next day, but still to no avail: nobody knew what had happened to the film, it was the governor's province, and he was at a ministerial conference. On the following day he finally got through.

'The film? Didn't it turn up? Well, that *is* strange… no, I knew nothing about it. Of course they can't always guarantee delivery you know… you mean somebody said that *I* said… no, I think somebody must have his wires crossed there. I tell you what, leave it with me – I'll get on to it and see that it's ready for next week… Goodbye, and keep up the good work.'

Honest or false? wondered Andrew. But the following week – still no film. That was the last time Andrew turned up. Crushed, a failure, he wandered absentmindedly out across the prison courtyard, acutely aware of guilt but longing to be free of the place for good. For some reason, when he got to the gate, he told the guard, 'I've given up teaching here; they're a hopeless lot of bastards, and they don't want to know anything.'

The guard shook his head sadly, 'I'm sorry to 'ear you say that,' he answered, 'they need good teachers in 'ere; most of them missed out on a decent education. If you ask me that's the main thing wrong with 'em.'

About six months later Andrew was hailed in Broad Street by a familiar voice. He was coming out of a bookstore, where he'd been treating himself to a pile of new paperbacks. He wheeled about and there, swaggering towards him, was the grinning figure of Stearns.

He considered running, but it was too late; Stearns was upon him. 'Well fancy bumping into you Teach. Sorry, I've forgotten your name…'

'Andrew. Andrew Elliot. When did you get out? What have you been doing?'

'Oh, this and that. Been out about two months now. What are you doing?'

'Oh, I've been, um, buying a few books…'

'Aah… you're a great one for the books. But I'll tell you somethin' Andrew; we really appreciated your book classes in there you know. Really appreciated 'em. A breath of fresh air in that stinking hole of a place. I'm never goin' back there again, that's for sure.'

Andrew had been expecting the familiar mocking tone, but he was surprised, and pleased, to find it absent. The voice was friendly, matey, and that mouth not nearly so truculent.

'That wasn't the impression I got at the time… I ended up thinking you all hated me.'

'Oh, no, no. That's not right. We appreciated you, really… but some of these blokes are a bit thick, you've got to expect that. But they like you… no, they *admired* you.'

Andrew felt a flicker of warmth for Stearns. Perhaps he had misjudged, and perhaps he had given up too soon. Stearns moved in a little closer to him and made his voice more confidential. 'Listen,' he said, 'you wouldn't have a couple of quid you could lend me would you?'

Little, cunning, criminal bastard, thought Andrew. So this is why he's buttering me up, this is what he wanted as soon as he saw me. To get something out of me, to make a fool of me yet again. He stood clutching his books and thought of the wad of notes in his pocket that he'd withdrawn from the bank only a few minutes earlier, and then he very casually lied, 'No I wouldn't actually, I'm sorry. As a matter of fact I haven't got a cent on me.' Then he reeled away quickly and lost himself in the walkers along the footpath, with as much elation in his heart as would have felt if he'd rammed his fist into that smirking, hateful mouth.

We All Make Them

It always eluded my self-understanding that I agreed to marry Alec. We were totally unsuited, with nothing in common except our love of music. I've often said it was because we were both so lonely at the time, which is true, but there was more to it than this. Something about his particular loneliness, and a deep need to be loved, called upon me to come to the rescue, which, while true enough, was I suppose also self-serving. I saw the chance to turn a man's life from miserable to happy, and in doing so raise my own self-esteem from abject to something better. But for all this high-minded intention, the enterprise was always doomed to fail.

This was in the late 1930s, the last stage of the Depression, and I was still getting over a dismal affair with a married man. I'd been living at home in Williamstown with my parents and three of my nine siblings, among whom I was the youngest, and just beginning to feel the need to break away and make a life of my own. My just-completed Classics degree fitted me for no kind of work I wanted to do, and I had no definite plans for a career. I talked to my sister Cass about it, brilliant Cass who always had such a clear sense of direction, already a partner in a firm of architects, passionate about her work, her clothes, her social circle, setting standards I couldn't hope to match, though I never resented her. Cass said, 'Why don't you write stories for magazines? You're a good writer, you showed that at uni.'

And I did start putting together some stories. The problem was, I quickly ran out of ideas to write about. I was honest enough with myself to realise I didn't know anything, hadn't really done anything, hadn't been anywhere. I had my favourite writers – George

Eliot, Edith Wharton, Scott Fitzgerald *et al* – and hoped they might serve as models. But all I could do was write about my own family, my own limited experiences, and I didn't dare offer them to anyone to read, let alone publish. So, I stuffed them in a folder in a drawer and forgot about them. What I needed, I announced to my family, was an income and a job that was compatible with my principles, and my brother Rob said, 'Stop being a dreamer Betty. The best plan for you is a shorthand and typing course at a city business college.' I always took what my siblings said seriously, so I enrolled and completed a six-month course at Taylor's in Little Collins Street.

My first job was in the office of an insurance firm, which was where I met Clarrie, one of the senior sales representatives. I typed letters for him, he chatted warmly with me, and I liked his confident, good-humoured personality, his smart suits and white shirts (god, I was so impressionable), but I had no illusions about his intellectual standards, or for that matter the nature of his interest in me. Yet, late one Friday afternoon when he asked me to go for a drink after work, I agreed. We went to a pub in the city, he bought me a brandy alexander and spun me the standard line of his wife 'not understanding him'; I wasn't stupid, and thought to myself 'No, I'll bet she understands you perfectly', but even so I agreed to let him drive me home. Instead of taking me straight to my house he drove to a quiet spot overlooking the beach and reached across and kissed me. When he put his hand inside my blouse I didn't protest. Again, without really understanding why, I allowed this to become a regular event, sometimes several times a week. And then one warm summer evening, with the sun low over the western suburbs, he took me to a secluded park near the river, we settled on the grass with his jacket over us, and as I lay silent beneath him he pushed up my skirt, removed my white satin underpants, entered me and told me I was 'miraculous'. I almost laughed out loud, but didn't. In his brusque way he was careful not to inseminate me; I felt torn about this –

partly grateful I would not get pregnant, partly resentful to be left unsatisfied, awkwardly cleaning up his mess on my stomach with my handkerchief. I was getting a numbing education in *coitus interruptus*, a phrase that, I later mused, had oddly enough not turned up in my Latin primer. Clarrie's 'miraculous', just like his constant talk of his conquests over women, colleagues, enemies and clients, was of course largely bullshit. And despite his complaints about his wife, he was never going to leave her or even tell her of our affair. It was all a dismal business, reducing me to a melancholy, guilt-ridden and even more lonely young woman than I'd been before. At least at university I had friends I could talk to, and the boys respected your intelligence, but all Clarrie did was use me.

It was, as I said, the final years of the Depression, and I came to wonder if that word, which was on everyone's lips, was about me personally. I tried talking to my mother about my feelings, but got nowhere; I simply had no language to tell her how it felt to be sexually frustrated, and why I was allowing myself to be used by a shitbag like Clarrie, because I didn't even know myself. Despite this, she knew there was something going on, and she would keep chipping away with unsubtle hints about 'what young girls get up to these days'. Finally, when I was laid low with the 'flu, she came into my bedroom to bring me a glass of orange juice, sat on my bed and grabbed the opportunity to paint the dramatic scene she'd been building up to for months. 'If a girl loses her virtue she loses the most precious thing she has... the man will have his pleasure of her then throw her in the gutter like a squeezed-out lemon... no other man will want to marry her...', on and on until I could have screamed and just wanted her out of the room. That was what finally decided me to move out of home and find myself an apartment.

Into the picture at that moment came Alec Debenham. He was a football club friend of my brother Rob, and in their teens he used to come to the house from time to time, before he and Rob went off to football. Walking along Collins Street one lunchtime, who should I bump into but Alec. By this time I had found a job in a Law firm, typing again, and had moved into a little place in East Melbourne, just a bedsitter with a kitchenette. Alec was excited to see me, and with footpath crowds brushing past us, we stood while he talked non-stop, breathlessly but self-effacingly, about how dreary it was living out in Camberwell with his mother, Ivy, how he hated his clerical job in advertising, and how unhappy he was with his life. I saw then how very different he was from Clarrie, with nothing of the predator about him at all. He politely walked me to my place of work, and then later that afternoon he rang me at the office and asked if I'd have dinner with him. He'd forgotten to mention, he said, it was his 21st birthday. Coming from a large family, I found this shocking – that someone could have absolutely no-one to celebrate their coming-of-age with, and that he hadn't even thought to mention it while we were walking. I agreed to meet him at seven o'clock in the foyer of the Hotel Australia in Collins Street.

When I got there he was already waiting for me, even though I was not late. He said he had worked out exactly where he would like to take me, which was a quiet basement restaurant in Little Collins Street, where he'd once or twice had lunch. The place had a dim, understated classiness about it, with its gleaming white tablecloths and napkins, its dark polished chairs and tables, and pleasant aroma of fish and coffee. We ordered lobster and the least expensive wine, and Alec told me that when he'd gone back to work that afternoon he'd felt lonely and a bit desolate, and thought, 'What would I like best in the world?' The answer came to him straight away, and he was prepared to risk it and pick up the phone. The fact was, he said, he'd worshipped me from afar ever since that day Rob had taken him home for a meal and he'd sat at our kitchen table almost too scared to look at me and thinking I was the most beautiful girl he'd ever seen. 'You were so intelligent and sparkling, and considerate too, the way you took the trouble to ask me about my family and interests; when I said that I had no father, you said 'That must have been hard on your mother, but she seems to have done a pretty good job,' I felt for the first time in my life that I was worth something'. He was smitten, but had believed that I, being a couple of years older than him, would never be interested in his meagre offerings. And yet now, against all the odds, here I was, his for the evening, at least.

I sensed that his lack of confidence meant I would have to make the running if anything was to come of our meeting. This was where I made my first mistake, or at least misjudgement. It was a matter of how the particular mix of two personalities can blind both to the folly of their actions. He interpreted my willingness for experience as evidence of his own unexpected desirability. I interpreted his lack of confidence as sensitive masculinity, which made him attractive. I discovered later that it was the way Alec always related to women: neediness was disguised as respect, possessiveness expressed as desire, or even love. Over the years women, or at least the ones he picked, couldn't help but respond to his insecurity, educated as we are to healing, nursing, mothering, caring. Equally, he couldn't seem to live without the quest for those very qualities in a woman, yet too often despising them when he found them. It was partly his looks, too: beautiful in some respects, with his thick dark hair, definite eyebrows, unmarked skin and mild grey eyes, all contriving to express a sadness that echoed back through his life, right from early childhood. To certain kinds of women he seemed the right material to work a transformation with, shaping him into the man they wanted. And I guess at that time in my life I must have been one of those very women.

After the meal we went to my East Melbourne flat, and a happy Alec immediately spotted my record collection on the shelves beside the double bed (in mentioning that bed now I can see what people mean when they describe me as having a 'strategic cast of mind'). The gramophone stood beside that. I was very proud of that electric gramophone, at a time when most people were still using mechanical ones. It was given to me as a graduation gift by my oldest brother David, the lawyer, who encouraged my interest in music, and had paid for piano lessons through my teens. Alec sat on the two-seat sofa while I sat on the bed, and together we listened to Artur Schnabel work his masterly way through the Beethoven Piano Sonata number 14, and me jumping up every few minutes to turn over the record. The sound, Alec said, was just as good as if it were coming over the wireless. The feelings between us were strange; I could sense his awkwardness and intimidation at being with me, but he was also emboldened by my obvious attempts to please him; I found myself opening to him, encouraging him. The shared experience of the music, and the unplanned nature of the whole day, made the evening special for us both. This feeling was even stronger when Alec found another, completely different, record on the shelf – Gladys Moncrieff singing 'Vilia' from *The Merry Widow*. I promptly put it on the gramophone, and we held our breath through the agonising seconds of static before the music began. As the voice moves through the opening verses, building expectations like the foundation of some great and beautiful monument, the breathless listener waits for the tune of the chorus to arrive, as it finally does in all its gentle yearning, and then feels as though her heart will burst with the swell of melancholy, at the same time separating her from everything except this passion that reaches on and out beyond and embraces nothing less than an infinite world. Only when the last tones of the song had died away did we move again, and Alec allowed himself a heavy sigh that sounded like relief, but was actually the language of wonder, 'Whoo…' he said, throwing me a brief look of appreciation. We turned to each other, two small souls needing a defence against such power, sensing that we might, in some unimaginable setting, be overwhelmed by it. We sought that defence in each other.

I took him to bed, and in the morning we agreed we were in love. From the wall phone in the hall we both rang our offices to say we were sick, and then we took ourselves back to bed. 'You're so beautiful,' he told me, 'and you're mine; you're *mine*!' After spending most of the morning between the sheets talking, loving, consuming toast and tea, we went down to St. Kilda ('we'd better not hang around the city in case someone from work sees us,' he said), walked along the beach in the cold June sunlight, and then found ourselves standing in the entrance mouth of Luna Park. 'Will we?' Alec said. 'Why not?' said I, and we spent an hour riding The Ghost Train, The Big Dipper, eating ice creams and playing the amusement stalls. After that we went to see *Goodbye Mr Chips* at the Palais Theatre; I enjoyed it especially because Mr. Chips was a Latin teacher, and Alec because he liked Robert Donat. We were both teary-eyed at the finish. Four weeks later Alec asked me to marry him, and to my own astonishment, I agreed.

Our families were told immediately. We took the train out to Camberwell so he could introduce me to his mother, the dreaded Ivy, and on the way Alec tried to prepare me for what I was about to confront. 'Don't be intimidated by her,' he said, 'she can be a bit eccentric, but she is essentially kind-hearted, and I'm sure you'll get on well.' All sorts of imaginings were going through my head when he said this, and were only compounded when he started filling me in on the family background. Whirlwind marriages leave a lot to catch up with, some of which might not take place for years, but at least Alec was trying to give me the general picture. 'I should tell you, too, that when you see the house it might look like there's a lot of family money, but unfortunately there isn't; my father's tribe were western district graziers, well-off before the First War, but something went wrong in the nineties and they had to sell off a lot of land. My grandfather had hoped my father would be able to build it up again, but that hope was all crushed when my father was killed on the Western Front. That virtually did my grandfather in, but he was able to buy the Camberwell house and provide well enough for my grandmother and my mother and her sister before he died a couple of years after the War. Unfortunately the income has been steadily going down over the years, reduced to a trickle by the Depression of course, and now there is virtually only the house and Ivy's War widow's pension.'

'But your mother paints, doesn't she?' I recalled it coming up at some point.

'Oh, yes, she certainly does,' he replied in a tone of near-exasperation, 'she certainly does. It's more important to her than anything else in the world, that and her Eltham artist friends. Not that she makes any money from it; she's lucky if she even gets a notice in the newspaper, when she's even allowed to exhibit her work, that is. It's hard for women to get shown in galleries. The group of artists she belongs to is better than most, in at least letting her show along with the men.'

We walked the short distance from the station to the house; and then I was overwhelmed by what I saw. It was one of those grand late Victorian mansions set in a large garden, overgrown from neglect, but obviously once carefully tended, judging by the wonderful array of trees and shrubs – rhododendrons, azalias, foxgloves, ferns and cycads, with the occasional bright rose breaking up the fustian, all competing for space. An oak and various ashes shadowed one side of the house, and a large jacaranda that would look stunning in bloom over the summer. The house itself was darkly imposing in its elevated position, built in deep red brick with green painted trim at the gables and verandas, a massive and complicated terracotta-tiled roof, and a definite suggestion of menace in its shadowed recesses.

'So this is where I grew up,' he said, as we entered through the massive front door. I wondered what effect growing up in such a place might have had on him. Was he happy here, or what? He'd answered the question before I had a chance to ask.

'I can't wait to get out and live somewhere else.'

'Really, but I would have loved to grow up in a house like this – so much space, so grand…'

'No – it's cold and dark. If it didn't actually cause my asthma, it certainly used to bring it on pretty often. Anyway, come and we'll tackle mother, and I'll show you around.'

Alec said she was eccentric, and I quickly got an inkling of what he meant. We'd been in the house a good fifteen minutes, wandering down its wide hallway, past its several dim sitting rooms, while Alec called out 'Ho-ome', showed me some of the numerous paintings by Ivy and some of her Eltham friends, before she appeared wearing paint-spattered men's khaki overalls and Wellington boots. The thing you noticed first about her was her high, protruding forehead, pronounced enough to give her a scary, slightly monstrous appearance. Her hair was tied up in a top-knot, but some of it fell in dark wisps over her flushed cheeks, and she greeted me with a handshake and a very other-worldly tone in her voice. She would have been in her mid-forties, but a lean, stringy energy in her movements made her seem younger.

'I'm sorry, I didn't hear you come in,' she said, 'Lost in a painting. I'll just get back to it if you don't mind, but I'll come and have some coffee with you in a little while,' and she moved to leave.

I was keen to see her at work if she'd let me, so I asked, 'Do you mind if I come and watch?'

She stood silent for a few moments, staring at me as if she hadn't understood what I'd said. Finally, she spoke, 'Well, I don't mind I suppose, if you can bear the boredom. Please don't speak while I'm working. And I, of course, won't speak to you.'

'Oh, I understand that. It's just that I've never seen anyone actually painting, and I'd love to see how you go about it.'

'I'll make some tea,' said Alec.

I followed her into what would probably have been a sunroom in the past, but was now set up as a studio, with the light streaming through the row of windows, brightening a junkyard of worked-on canvases propped up against walls, easels bearing unfinished ones, tables covered in squashed paint tubes, vases and jars holding brushes, plaster models of heads and figurines, and everything well-used and spattered with paint. I loved the smell and feel of it, and the atmosphere of work it evoked.

She set about an already begun streetscape, and seemed to be using a thinning liquid to brush over all the edges of objects, making them blurred and misty. It was as if she wanted the features to be seen through a light fog, so that the dark trees, the grey road carrying it's black squared-off motor car, the highlights of bright colour representing traffic and street lights, simplified to their basics, all took on an ethereal lyricism that was a bit like the woman herself.

Afterwards we had tea at the big oak table in the old country-style kitchen, its walls all white-tiled in the Victorian half-off-set style, though some were looking the worse for wear. It was weird and coldly isolating having such a huge house with such huge rooms for two people. And it can't have been cheap to maintain, with rates, and heating and such. I wondered if she thought of moving to a smaller place after Alec left.

'Where would I go?' she said, 'Anyway, I expect you two will want to move in here after the wedding, won't you?'

'No, not a bit of it,' Alec said, 'too far from work. Betty's got a flat in East Melbourne we can stay in for a while, till we find something else.'

'Well I can't say I'm unhappy about that; I'm not much fun to live with these days, and in any case it's time you made a life for yourself. You'll do fine in East Malvern or wherever it is.' She looked at me:

'Are you pregnant?' she asked.

'No, I'm not,' I laughed.

'Just as well; this is no time to be bringing children into the world.'

I wasn't sure what she meant by 'this is no time', so I just mindlessly said, 'No, I don't suppose it is,' and let it go at that. She could have been referring either to the Depression, which hadn't then come to an end, or to the prospect of the coming War, which was on everyone's lips. Or both.

Going back in the train I said to Alec, 'She's not so much eccentric as anti-social, is she?'

'To be honest, I've never been able to figure out what she is. You can probably tell that there are few displays of affection between us. Not the usual mother-and-son type. I'll be surprised if she turns up at the wedding, or even remembers that it's happening.'

In the weeks leading up to the wedding Alec and I spent a lot of time together. We kept working until the last day before my notice ended and his leave began, and so we'd have lunch together, usually on the grassy Yarra bank near Princes Bridge, often meeting after work for dinner, or go back to my flat and I'd cook something. He'd either go home to Camberwell on the train, or stay the night with me. Mostly, they were lovely times, despite the Depression, and if I'd not been so busy with wedding plans, and blinded by optimism, I'd have taken more notice of a couple of worrying signs. The first was his oversensitivity to criticism; any suggestion that he might be wrong about something could set him off in a bitterly dark mood. The second was his inexplicable tendency to self-pity, inexplicable that is until he indicated its source one night. Talking late into the night in bed, and still under the influence of the wine he'd drunk after dinner, he revealed a disturbing situation about his childhood.

'I should never have been born,' he said.

'What do you mean?'

'I don't believe I was wanted. I think Ivy would have been happier without having to bring me up.'

I was at a loss to respond. It was a dreadful thing to say, but there was no point trying to resist it; if he felt it, he felt it. But why?

'Well, for a start, I've always felt I was adopted. That she never gave birth to me.'

'Why would you think that?'

'She never showed me any affection. Never cuddled me, or kissed me. In fact, she always gave me the impression she couldn't bear to touch me. I felt completely unwanted.'

'That must have been awful for you,' I reached out and clasped his hand. 'Why would you have been unwanted?'

'I don't know. I grew up seeing how differently other children were treated – how they were taken on holidays, how they were included and fussed over by their parents, how they spent *time* with them. When I wasn't at school I was always on my own – given a playroom crammed with toys and left to get on with it. And even at school there was always my asthma; that stopped me getting into sport with the other boys…'

'Maybe she had her reasons.'

'If she did, she didn't make them clear to me.'

'It doesn't mean you were adopted. She was bringing you up alone of course – that might have affected her. What about your father?'

'Killed at the Somme. All I know is his name was Justin, and that he was gassed.'

But she would never tell me about him, and I grew up accepting that I wasn't supposed to ask. The whole subject was a closed door.'

'Well there you are then; that's got to be her reason. Shock, trauma, of a kind she's never been able to get over. You must have been just a baby, and she not long married. To lose him like that would have been devastating. There's your explanation: you remind her of the pain of losing him.'

'For twenty years? And it wasn't *my* fault!'

'She knows that, and she no doubt isn't blaming you; but her feelings have somehow been frozen into a kind of permanent state I suppose. Not that it helps you any to see that.'

'No, it doesn't. But it's why I've always felt she didn't want me. Her *painting* is more important to her than I've ever been.'

Of course, his telling me this only brought out my own foolish instinct to love him more, and to try to make up for those years of deprivation. What I didn't see, or couldn't see, in these early days together, was the way in which he could use this feeling – this protective instinct – to undermine my genuine affection for him. That didn't become evident until some while after we'd been married.

Since neither of us was interested in religion, we planned to marry at the city Registry Office in the middle of August, 1939. My mother was bitterly disappointed that we didn't choose a church, and she and my father stubbornly refused to attend. Mum was convinced no good could come of a union made in such a hurry and without the blessing of an Anglican vicar. Nevertheless, she reminded me that we would still be watched over by a caring, if sadly un-denominated, Power, which struck me more as a threat than a promise.

Ivy, for her part, was indifferent to religion, and as it turned out she did actually come to the Registry Office service. But a few days before the event she dropped an extraordinary weight of knowledge in our laps, or to be precise, in my lap, at least in the first instance. In her response to the wedding invitation I'd sent, a note arrived in the post, which read:

My Dear Betty (or should it be Elizabeth?),

First, I do plan to be at the wedding, thank you, and I'm glad that you are getting married quickly. Some would warn against such haste, but like Lady Bracknell, I do not believe in long engagements, especially in these uncertain times, when anything might happen. I'm only glad that Alec has found a woman who is prepared to take him on, and I trust you will both be very happy together. Certainly, I wish it may be so.

And I also want to speak to you on another matter, but one that I'm not able to relate to you properly in writing. It concerns Alec, and refers to matters that should be passed on to you sooner rather than later. To this end, may I visit you this Thursday morning at 11 o'clock? Ring me on 524336 if the time and day are not suitable.

Yours in good faith,

Ivy Debenham (Mrs)

I still have this letter somewhere amongst my things; I put it away safe because think I already guessed that it marked a significant event. As it happened, the day she suggested was not especially convenient – I was still in a panic trying to organise the reception lunch and my clothes for going away – but I nevertheless rang and told her it would be okay to come as proposed. I had by that time left my job, giving myself barely a week to get everything done. But I was at least free.

She arrived by taxi, and once again her appearance was memorable. She was wearing a black cloche hat and a long black straight coat with a fur collar, like she'd just turned up for a 1920s funeral fifteen years too late. She came into my bedsit, and when she removed her hat and coat, revealing a dark blue patterned low-slung frock and sturdy shoes, the image of outdated fashion was complete, like an ageing flapper. My heart went out to her in that moment, because I could see that her whole social sense was sadly rooted in the distant past, and what was worse, she didn't seem to know it. I made some tea and tried to forget about her appearance. Settling into my sofa, while I sat opposite her on the bed, she launched into her story.

'I want you to know about Alec,' she began, 'because unless you do your marriage might not have much chance of success.' She was of course blithely unaware that my own mother had all but given up any hope of that ever happening.

For someone whose main way of addressing the world was visual, she talked well and to the point, sometimes brusquely, as one who can't bear to waste time on chit-chat, and so I was pleased that she got straight to her subject. 'He's always had difficulty relating to women,' she said, 'intrigued by them, eager to pursue them, but desperately insecure about their feelings for *him.*'

'I'd gathered that much for myself.' I said, resisting the impulse to explain how.

She took a sip of her tea, and clutched the saucer on her lap with her free hand. I couldn't help noticing her unusually short, strong looking fingers, a man's fingers I thought, made for practical use.

'It was my fault, of course,' she said, lowering the cup, 'The fact is that having been gifted him, I found it difficult to take an interest in him. I suppose motherhood is not my thing, though with Alec I had a reason, which has taken me almost a lifetime to come to terms with.'

That phrase 'motherhood is not my thing' struck me as jarringly offhand, yet I believed it was honest and unrehearsed; I saw that Ivy was not at all used to laying herself open like this, and that she was attempting to exorcise demons that had long troubled her.

'But you must have been so busy, with your painting as well as a child to rear…?'

'Busy? Oh yes, I've been busy. I don't know what I'd have done if I'd not had my painting. It was a very lucky day indeed the day I met Mister Meldrum…'

'Mister Meldrum…?'

'Mister Max Meldrum, the painter and teacher. I was just a Sunday painter before I met him, repeating pretty much what I'd learned as a schoolgirl at *The Hermitage.*'

'You grew up in Geelong? I didn't know that.'

'Alec hasn't told you? You must be a very brave girl, or a foolhardy one, to marry him without going into his family background. I was a Colac girl, but they sent me to Geelong for my schooling, and I used to come home to help my father in his accountancy business in school holidays. My husband's family were Western District graziers, and if he hadn't died at the Somme I suppose that's what was in store for me – farmer's wife.'

'And after the War, you went up to Camberwell to live with your sister?'

'I wanted to get away from everything that reminded me of Justin, and Winsome had our big old house that I'd always loved.'

'And that's when you met Mister Meldrum?'

'I started painting lessons at the National Gallery School, but I wasn't happy there, then I heard about this charismatic rebel who had his own theory of painting, and decided try him out. He not only changed my technique; he changed my life. Anyway, let's not go into that now. That's not what I came to talk to you about. I want to tell you about Alec. In fact, I want to tell you who he is, which is something he doesn't even know himself.'

She paused here, which I couldn't tell how much was done for effect, or from a last-minute reluctance to say what she had come to say. She looked down at her hands, and almost rushing the words, said, 'Alec is actually an adopted child.'

'My goodness Ivy; do you know that Alec has always *felt* he was adopted? He told me only recently…'

'Well, I'm not surprised… but anyway please don't interrupt me; this is difficult enough.'

'Sorry.'

But she slowed her words all the same, lifted her head and resumed with a note of defiance in her voice. 'When I married Justin it was a marriage of true minds, and we were very much a young country couple in love. God I adored that boy! He was so handsome and gentle, not a mean fibre in his body.'

I loved hearing her say this; it was the first time I actually warmed to her, and caught a glimpse into feelings that had been suppressed for a lifetime. I felt ashamed that I had been dismissing her as merely 'eccentric'. She continued, 'When the War came he was determined to enlist and, like many others, to do his bit for the Mother Country; his family was very pro-British – his father referred to England as Home right up to his death, despite sixty-odd years in this country. So Justin enlisted and while we waited to hear when he was likely to be shipped off to France, we decided to marry before he left. There was some agonising over this – Justin was concerned that I could be left in circumstances that would make it difficult for me to marry again should anything happen to him. But I was insistent – I wanted us to make love while we could – and if it resulted in us producing a child, so much the better.

'The wedding had been arranged for December, 1916, on the assumption, based on an educated guess from a Department of Defence source, that it was unlikely he would be shipped off before Christmas. Of course, no one can predict army decisions, and in October Justin received a letter telling him to present himself at Victoria Barracks on October 20th in preparation for embarkation the following day – months before we expected! That put the cat among the pigeons, I can tell you. My mother was running around rearranging invitations, seeing to the Banns, booking venues in Geelong. Juggling all these problems meant that the best we could do was to get married on the 19th – that is, the day before he had to leave. We had one night together, and that was it, next day he would be gone to God-knows what horrors on the Western Front.

'And then another eventuality, this time a disastrous one. The day before the wedding Justin was given his inoculations against typhoid and smallpox. They made him sick. He had a fever during the service, and afterwards, in the hotel in Melbourne where we spent our only night together before he shipped off, he couldn't eat his dinner and virtually passed out in our room afterwards. I sat with him most of the night swabbing him down with damp cloths, trying to get his fever down. Needless to say, we were unable to…' She finished her tea and placed the cup on the table in front of her, then looked me straight in the eye, waiting for me to acknowledge her meaning.

I gave her the response she wanted. 'You were unable to make love?'

'That is, I suppose one would say, the gist of it. You will make of it what you will, my dear Betty, but I tell you something now that I have never told another soul: I was, and still am, a virgin.'

Whatever she expected, the fact is it didn't come as a complete surprise to me; there was in her whole taut bearing a sense that certain feelings and experiences had long been locked away, that she was permanently on guard against sentiments that might in some way coerce her. If I'm being a bit clever about it here, I would say that her capacity for love had not died, but had just been sublimated into her painting – let's face it, we're all Freudians now. But of course the big question hanging in my mind was one that I was sure she was coming to, though how long it might take I could only guess. So I got up and made another pot of tea, and found some biscuits to sustain us, and then I prompted her onwards.

'So how did Alec come into the picture?' I said. I think I was already presuming that some kind of compensatory action had taken place, that a childless wife widowed by the War would quite understandably resort to adoption when Nature had been so cruelly blasted out of the equation. She picked up her tea and bit into a biscuit before she went on.

'Justin wrote me letters almost every other day, especially in those first months. I received over a dozen written from the transport ship alone. They were beautiful, unforgettable letters, the thoughts of a sensitive boy discovering the big world out there – the sea, the exotic sights on the passage over, the friendships he would otherwise never have made. When he got to England, which was at first a time of boredom while they trained – he had been made a gunner in a trench mortar battery – he began to enjoy the lovely English countryside, the busy world of London – it was all in his letters. And when they finally got to France there were more awakenings – he started to learn the language, experience another country's ways – it was all a wonderland for him, although he never forgot the terrible purpose of it all, and never dismissed from his mind the ugly realities he would face. 'Inevitably, of course, he began to experience some of those realities, and he would indicate them in his letters, despite the censorship; you could read between the lines of cheerful lies that he was hating it all – the mud, the injuries, the gas, the noise of the guns, the deaths, the disgusting inhumanity. It was the horses that particularly upset him, being a country boy; he couldn't bear to see them killed, maimed, driven crazy by the explosions, being dragged into what was primarily a human debacle. That's what he called it in one letter: a human debacle; somehow the censor let that one through.'

'That would have affected me, too,' I said, 'you hear a great deal about the terrible sufferings of the men, but you don't hear much about the horses, or the dogs for that matter, simply used as if they were pieces of equipment…' My voice must have gone a bit emotional at this; Ivy finished her tea and stood up. 'I'm sorry if this is upsetting you, Betty,' she said, 'I haven't been thinking of your feelings in telling you all this, and just when you're trying to prepare for one of the happiest times in your life. Perhaps I should leave this story for another time…'

'No, no,' I protested, 'It's not upsetting me really. I want to know about Alec's father, and about you and how you managed through it all.'

'Well, first I need to use your lavatory – all this tea, you know…'

When she returned she seemed refreshed and less tense; she walked about the room, peeped into the kitchenette, looked at my meagre collection of books and records, and said, 'I see you're a music lover; that no doubt pleases Alec,' before finally dropping herself back on to the sofa, and resuming her story.

'His unit was sent to the region around Amiens, where there had been terrible fighting in the months before; they were doing a kind of clean-up, and there he got himself injured in a most absurd way; he apparently made some kind of 'mistake' loading a mortar, and lost the top joints of his middle and ring fingers. He was sent to a casualty station, and then on to hospital, where he stayed for several weeks to recuperate. That was in September, 1917. I know because that time, I've come to understand, was where the course of my life changed…'

I jumped in. 'He died there?'

'Oh no, dear Betty; he didn't die there. Quite the contrary. He started a new life there.'

'How?'

'It turns out he met a nurse, and they had what I suppose

people are happy to call an affair.' An ironic smile.

'He wrote and told you about it?' I asked.

'Oh no, he did not. In fact his letters became few and far between around this time. I put this down to the War and the uncertainties of the mail, but it turned out not to be the case. He simply had more interesting things to do than to write to me.'

'How did you find out, then?'

'Well, I didn't. Not then. I knew nothing about it at the time. Here we all were, worried sick that he'd been hurt or that something else dreadful had happened to him, and all the time he was swanning around in safe areas with his lady. No, I didn't know anything about it, and the next time I heard from him was months later in April when he wrote from an area near Passchendaele that there was a new push from the Germans causing some heavy fighting, and for me not to worry as his unit were not in the front line…'

She stopped for a moment, her emotions getting the better of her; the controlling tone was beginning to break down. I waited until, with her hand pressed to her chest, she quietly resumed.

'… and that was the last letter I had from him. The next news I got was that dreaded pink telegram from the Post-Master General, that he had been killed in action on the ninth of May near a little village called Rivery. It was later confirmed that he was one of a number in his unit who had been hit by mustard gas and died a few days later in a casualty station. God knows what suffering he endured in those few days.'

I still wondered how Alec's adoption came into the picture. All sorts of questions were bubbling in my head: surely if she was feeling angry at the end of the War, and bitter, which it seems she was, why would she then want to randomly adopt a child and raise him to believe that Justin was his father? And who was the mother? I was soon to learn.

My East Melbourne flat was part of an old house that had

once been a grand bungalow; I guess my room had been in the servants' or butler's quarters, and was tucked under a rear veranda looking out on quite a nice area of semi-formal garden – low shrub-hedging and stubby azaleas, and a very fetching magnolia in the centre of the lawn. When she'd finished telling me about her husband's death, Ivy stood at my lounge room window gazing out on that garden, the memories flooding in. I can still see her, dressed in those 1920s clothes, a figure frozen in time, absorbed still in the events she'd been talking of, resisting the pressure to rage or cry or laugh or to let her bitterness have its head, but simply and silently, and no doubt painfully, reliving them. I couldn't think of anything to say but, 'And Alec?'

She turned away from the window and sat down again. 'Yes, well that brings me to the whole point of telling you all this, doesn't it?' she said, 'Alec, and his auspicious arrival. I had not given a thought to the matter of children. Once I knew that Justin was gone it was irrelevant anyway. I loved him passionately; couldn't imagine marrying again, couldn't imagine anyone filling the hole he'd left in my life. I was simply sunk in grief, convinced I'd never feel happiness again. My parents tried to comfort me – I was still living in Colac with them at that time – and I tried to use my painting as a way of resisting self-pity, but my heart wasn't in it. I would stand at my easel and instead of painting the scene in front of me I would simply weep at it, and then retreat into my bedroom. All I could see of the months ahead of me was misery and loneliness. I would walk around the lake by myself and think about stepping off the pier into the water.

'And then, out of the blue, one day in December, a knock came on the front door. My mother answered it, and then called to me that there was a woman asking for me. When I walked into our sitting room there was this tall, dark-haired young woman holding a baby wrapped in a white shawl. She said her name was Emilia Lang, that the father of the baby she was holding was Justin, and that she'd come home in disgrace from France to give birth to it. I was struck completely dumb. Didn't know in that moment what to feel. What to think. And she had come prepared. She had the forethought to realise that she might not be believed, and that she might appear to be some unfortunate young woman who'd given birth out of wedlock and was looking to extort money out of a stranger – goodness knows how I thought such a person would know me or my circumstances – and so by way of proving the truth of her story she produced a letter from Justin, written to her at her Melbourne address in March 1918, just a couple of weeks after she left France to return to Australia big with his child, and only two months before he was killed. That letter was full of love and concern that was typical of Justin's particular brand of kindness, and as I read it through, it tore my heart out. In the final sentences he was promising to marry her, and to ask me for a divorce.

'I handed the letter back and looked her over. She wasn't beautiful, as if that mattered. It was clear she wasn't poor or destitute – a driver in a dark green touring automobile was waiting in the street in front of the house – and she hadn't come for any objectionable purpose; what she said, she said apologetically. 'It was my fault that it all happened,' she said, 'I should never have let things go as far as they did.' I said back to her, nodding towards the baby, 'And certainly, you should never have allowed *that* to happen; I thought a nurse would be more careful…' She had met him when he was in after-care after the operation on his hand, that he was not coping well with the loneliness, missing home and his family, including me too I suppose. 'People back home can't imagine what it's like over there, what everyone is going through,' she said, 'and the nurses saw the worst of it. Hearing grown men in the wards call for their mothers in the middle of the night. Bathing pathetic amputees, their stitches still fresh and weeping. Watching a boy you had joked with at breakfast fade and die during the afternoon. You come to feel that any moment of normal life should be grabbed while it's there. That any soldier you struck up a friendship with could be gone the next day.'

'And then she told how one day *it* began to happen between them, and this was the part that caused me the most pain. Not so much because he betrayed me; strangely I was able to understand something of his need for companionship and love in that horrific situation, and forgive his natural desire. After all, it was common for the soldiers to go to prostitutes, anyone knows that. No, it was that *I* had not been brave enough to do what *she* did with him. I regretted, and still regret, that Justin and I, when we were courting, didn't simply let our feelings have their full freedom, and to hell with the consequences.'

I broke in at these words, feeling I ought to say something to mitigate her regret. 'But well brought-up young girls didn't in those days, there was too much at stake, surely?'

'Oh yes, yes, we know all that don't we,' retorted Ivy. 'The fact remains that *carpe diem* is as strong an argument as it ever was, perhaps stronger. Especially back then.'

I was hardly in a position to dispute this, having been sleeping with Alec for over a fortnight now, indulging in exactly the premarital sex that Ivy had denied herself. I was eager to hear the rest of the story about Justin and this Emilia.

'You know,' she went on, 'I have often imagined them, my husband with this dark-haired nurse, conducting their affair in that war-torn world, the creaking beds in cheap rooms, the green riverside nooks they might have found to lie in, the snatched moments in dark corners of the hospital. I know it's a kind of masochism on my part, but it must have been so full of danger and passion. Much as I hated and resented what they had done, I had to admire her, if not for anything else, certainly for having the guts to go over there in the first place. They were out there, taking on the full force of the world, while I was stuck here in my little privileged cocoon. I felt then that she would have made him a more exciting wife than I ever could.

'Anyway, to come to the point, this Emilia stood before me, open in her admission that she had been Justin's lover, which she didn't regret, and that she had given birth to a boy, who was now six months old. Naturally I was shocked, and hurt and angry, too, I can't deny that. I was wondering why she had brought him all this way for me to see, wondering if she was driven by generosity of feeling or just mindless swagger, when suddenly she dropped her bombshell. 'I want you to have him,' she declared. 'I want you to bring him up… to be his mother.'

'I blurted out my immediate reaction,' Ivy continued, 'which was of course astonishment. I protested that the child had nothing to do with me… that I was in no position to take him and raise him as my own. But I could see she was trapped. She said that her family – a proud Toorak clan apparently – wouldn't countenance keeping him, arguing it would ruin her life, destroy her chances of marriage, which was probably true. So, she had agreed to put him out for adoption, and then somehow hit upon the idea of offering him to me. She had long known my address from my letters back to Justin; did she actually read them? I never knew. I could see that she was reluctant to go through with the whole formal adoption business, so we sat down and we talked, and out it all poured, the feelings that had grown between her and Justin in France, little details of things he said and did that reminded her of home, how his stories of growing up on the farm, his childhood adventures, how he longed always to be out in the paddocks regardless of the weather. As I listened to this my jealousy grew and my resentment deepened. This was *my* courtship she was describing, these were *my* experiences, and she had stolen them, only she had used them to enjoy the very sexual experience with him that I had not. I wanted to call her a whore, but the last thing I wanted was to lose control of the situation.

'All right,' I thought, 'you've done this one thing with him; but everything else the two of you felt, he felt with me first. So, yours was a second-hand affair; mine was the original.' Madness, I know, but jealousy can lead to bizarre thoughts. At this moment I detested her. At one point in the conversation she made a move to grasp my hand, but I pulled it away; she wanted to be friends. And in that moment I glimpsed the power that my position gave me. I would indeed take Alec and raise him as my own, enjoying taking him away from her, enjoying her abjectness. Because I did want some revenge. I told myself, and for years clung to the delusion, that she had been the mere pod that had carried Alec, and that really all along he was mine and Justin's, that when he had put his seed into *her* Justin had actually been inseminating *me*. He didn't love her, I told myself; she was merely the convenient surrogate for me, the one love of his life that he had freely chosen, not driven to it by the privations of War, as he had with her.

'Then the baby needed feeding, and she brought out a bottle and nursed it on her lap while he fed. When she offered me a turn, I overcame my first instinct to refuse, and agreed to hold him. I was pleased to let her show me how to go about it, and again I was enjoying the sense that she was experiencing some pain, even if it was mixed with a certain sense of the virtue of sacrifice. 'He's called Alec,' she said, 'after my grandfather.' Holding him, watching him suck on the bottle, my confidence in being able to look after him grew; I began to think there was a mother in me somewhere. 'Hello little Alec,' I mooned, and I could see my way to presenting him to the world as my own child, and no-one need ever know the real story behind his birth. I was sure my parents and other family and close friends would go along with the story. And they did. The adoption never went through the authorities, was never made formal. I simply called him a Debenham – which of course is not biologically wrong – though his birth certificate will say something else; Lang I suppose.

That is something he might find out if ever he has to apply for it.'

'So you accepted him, as you said before,' I said, 'I know now what you meant when you said he was 'gifted' to you. He really was literally a gift. And tell me Ivy, what happened to Emilia? I've certainly never heard mention of her until now.'

'Oh, that was another peculiarity. After she waved to me from that green automobile as it pulled away from our house, I never saw or heard from her directly again. She'd promised to write, and even to visit from time to time, but she never did. I thought of chasing her up, but then I realised there was no point. I would guess her family had intervened, and did whatever was necessary to keep her from having any further contact with Alec or me. They wanted that chapter of her life closed, and to help her find a way of beginning again. That was fine – it suited me. But I do know she managed to marry – about two years after the War there was a notice and photograph in the society pages of the Melbourne *Argus*; the full white wedding at St. John's church in South Yarra, the beaming groom no doubt entirely unaware of the shady past and certain censure that his bride had narrowly escaped.'

'Crikey, Ivy,' I said, 'what an astonishing story. And despite what you say about your feelings towards her, it was still a brave and generous thing to do, taking on the job of raising a child fathered by your husband on another woman.'

'Well,' she said circumspectly, 'I take a different view of it now. I should never have done it. Even with the best of intentions one doesn't necessarily end up with perfect results, and my intentions were never the best. He would probably have done better with his mother, or even formally adopted by another woman, I'm sure. I learned the hard way I was not cut out to be a mother. I hated the relentless crying, the loss of sleep, the feeds at four in the morning. I'd hoped it might have been a consolation to remember that he was Justin's child, but it turned out to be no help; he was just a constant reminder of his father's betrayal, and the destruction of all my hopes and dreams of living a happy married life after the War. Not only did I lose my husband: I lost his love, which was as bad; I couldn't even cling to the belief that he died thinking of me. He probably didn't. And it didn't help that Alec was a rather unprepossessing child – sickly, asthmatic, whingy and clingy. He wasn't particularly bright, couldn't play sport because of his health. I'm afraid I found him difficult to love, and I'm not proud of that. As I say, I was not cut out for motherhood, and I did a bad job of it, once I came under the wing of Mister Meldrum. He encouraged me to see the world differently, to understand it as a visual composition, and from then on I wanted to be an artist above everything else. My sister Winsome, thank goodness, was able to step in much of the time, and give Alec the attention I failed to give, until she died when he was nine. With painting the main focus of my life, Alec was mostly left to his own devices, I'm afraid. He was always fed and clothed, of course, and was sent to a good school, but I know he never received the affection he wanted, and deserved. And I'm sorry about that, I truly am, but there it is.'

'I'm so glad you've told me all this,' I said, 'It will help me to understand Alec better, and might help us in living together, I'm sure…'

'But that's not the main reason I'm telling you,' she interrupted. 'I'm telling you because I want *you* to tell Alec the truth about his mother, and the circumstances of his parenting.'

'But surely you should do it? It would mean more coming from you…'

But she was insistent. It was too late for her to tell him now, it would only seem like self-justification, an excuse for her selfishness and neglect. She couldn't do it. So, I agreed to try, but I was not confident about his reaction. She was asking me to do something she should have done many years earlier – when he finished primary school perhaps, and he would be old enough to understand but still young enough to adjust his emotional expectations. But she had preoccupied herself with her painting, reordering the way the world looked, adding to her son's lack of a father by virtually depriving him of a mother as well. You only get one shot at parenting each child, and if you blow it, the ground is irrecoverable. As I've often thought about our mistakes in life, and have come to the view that we all need to be doing things for the second time. If only it were possible.

Ivy stood up and collected her coat from where I'd placed it on the back of a chair in the kitchen. I didn't know at that point whether to be grateful or dismayed by the things she's told me. I doubt she'd ever told it to anyone else, though I suppose her sister Winsome would have known some things first hand. Their parents were long dead by then, and the one person who should have been told had been left all those years in ignorance of the truth. It wasn't my place to condemn her, but I thought that Alec certainly would when I told him.

'It's coming up lunch time,' I said to her, 'I have some reasonably fresh bread and a bit of cheese if you'd like to stay for a bite.' But she declined, and said it was only a short walk to the tram in Wellington Parade, and it wasn't a particularly inclement day. I offered to walk with her.

'No, not a bit of it,' she said, 'I'm used to it,' she said, 'I'm out in the weather most days now, on my bicycle, towing its little box trailer with my easel and paints; it gives me a good long day making use of the light, having the bike. No, I'll be fine.'

And she left me, still struggling to come to terms with the task she'd given me, three days before I was due to marry Alec. And which I was now charged with laying on him. How would he take it? I just hoped I could get the story across to him without bringing on another one of his black depressions.

He was coming to eat with me that Thursday evening before going home to Camberwell afterwards; we had decided it felt a little more decorous to sleep separately until after the wedding, which I know was a weird and somewhat hypocritical attitude to take, but it did sort of feel right. I dashed out and bought a nice piece of smoked cod, a not-too-cheap bottle of riesling, and whipped up an apple pie, all of which were favourites with him, in the hope of putting him in a good mood for what I was going to be telling him.

Talk about anti-climax! He arrived a little late, because he'd gone to Allen's Music Shop on the way and bought a new recording of the Mendelssohn E minor Violin Concerto, was looking forward to playing it on my gramophone, thus he was already upbeat when he walked in. We opened the wine and he sat listening to the music while I prepared the meal, and as we ate I told him about Ivy's visit, which truly astonished him, and relayed everything she'd told me about his father, the relationship with Emilia, his birth, and his adoption. Through it all he concentrated his focus on eating, pushing food round the plate in a fussily organised routine, listening without interrupting me, and when I'd finished he poured the last of the wine into his glass and pushed back in his chair, looking composed and philosophical. His unexpected calm was somewhat of an antidote to the intensity of my retelling of the story, and I was very glad for the change.

'I told you so, didn't I?' he said, 'I always knew it. I always knew she wasn't my real mother. That stupid woman; she could have told me the truth right from the start, which at least would have saved me from the false expectations I had right through my childhood. All she did was make life that much more complicated, just to spare a few blushes on behalf of my dead father.'

'Not just that, of course,' I said, 'I think she had her own defences to maintain. What would it have said about *her* if she had declared you to be adopted, and that she was not your real mother?

The questions – 'why did he go to another woman?' 'What if she changes her mind and wants him back?' And she would have always looked like the second choice. From her point of view it was always simpler to pretend you were hers, rather than face prying questions.'

He got up from the table and went over to the gramophone, carefully placing the disks back in their brown paper sleeve and into the flat box that housed them. Meanwhile I served up the apple pie and put on some coffee. When he sat back down he said, 'This doesn't change anything for me, or for us. Except, I'll be interested to see what my birth certificate says when I go to the Registry Office, which I'll have to do tomorrow.'

'Which reminds me – I have to be getting on with things for Saturday. I've got some mending to do and a few other things – I lost a lot of time today because of Ivy. And tomorrow I have to go to the hotel and finalise the food arrangements.'

'Busy busy,' he said cheerfully, and reached his hand across the table to clasp mine. 'I'll go as soon I've had some coffee. Maybe we could go to the pictures tomorrow night?'

'You're joking,' I laughed, 'I still have a mountain of things to do.'

'We'll eat out then.'

'We'll see; I'll ring you I wonder how things will be between you and Ivy when you get home. What will you say to her? Now that her secret is out; *your* secret is out! How will you two regard each other now?'

'I really don't know; really don't know. Anyway, there's no point getting upset about it now; too much water under the bridge…'

'I'll be dying to hear all about it.'

At the wedding, Ivy came alone, wearing a white dress, again 1920s style, and large white hat with a small tulle veil, almost as if it was her own wedding she was attending. Alec had said she was 'eccentric', and I suppose this is true, but I've wondered if she's also some sort of archetype of the artist. She stood apart from everyone else until Cass (who actually owned one of her paintings), joined her outside the Registry Office and the pair chatted happily. Afterwards Ivy slipped away almost unnoticed, until someone pointed out that she was no longer around. A strange woman, not fitted for family life, and I would like to have seen her mixing with her artist friends just to see what she was like with her own kind.

Several of my brothers, including Sep and Rob, who gave me away, were there, along with sisters Jean and Cass, as distinctly secular-looking bridesmaids. Cass was wonderfully supportive, although it was clear to everyone that she didn't think much of Alec; but then it was always going to be hard to find anyone she thought good enough for her little sister. When Cass learnt that I intended to turn up in my one and only suit, which was black, she cried 'Not on your life!' and immediately whisked me out to the city shops and bought me a beautiful dress, matching coat, and a chic 'robin hood' style hat. I of course had to resign from my job, and when the ceremony was over the remains of the party went to a city hotel and lunched on chicken-in-a-basket, buttered asparagus and champagne (none of which were seen again until after the War). Afterwards, we set off with some luggage by train to Frankston, where we were to honeymoon for two weeks. It was a time of wintry, unsettled weather, with grey mornings that could often resolve into blue, breezy afternoons; we walked and talked, stayed whole mornings in bed, and made love at least once every day.

But by the end of the first month I knew in my heart it was all a mistake. Alec proved a very difficult man to live with. Moody, always moody. And given to paralysing fits of jealousy. Even at Frankston I had seen the signs. Sitting on beach with our clothes over our swimsuits that first morning, determined to act in holiday spirit in defiance of the winter temperature, and contemplating whether or not to fling ourselves into the waves, Alec suddenly asked, 'Am I a better lover than your last one?'

'What do you mean, "my last one"?' I laughed, 'You make it sound as though there's been an endless line of them.'

He gave a little snort. 'Well, you said yourself I'm not the first.'

'No, you're not, that's true. I told you that weeks ago. And you said it didn't matter. So why are you mentioning it now? Why is it bothering you?' I was hurt.

'I don't know, it just *is*.' This was said with a tinge of anger, the anger of self-justification, when you know you're on shaky ground and have to resort to counter-attack. He added, 'You don't… you *didn't*… seem at all disquieted at our making love…'

'Should I feel disquieted? Anyway, what does that even mean, feel disquieted? It was something I wanted, wanted to enjoy. I like sex, and I like it with you. What's wrong with that?'

He looked down, drawing circles in the sand with a twig he'd picked up.

'Did you like sex with Clarrie too?'

I didn't answer. Peremptorily, I rose from the towel, took off my pullover and slacks, stood in my blue one-piece swimsuit, and putting on my bathing cap, said 'I'm going for a swim,' and headed straight down to the water. I could feel him watching me go. I waded in up to my waist, then glided forward to disappear into the blue-green swell, then swam at least fifty yards, directly out to sea, and all the time knowing he was watching me and his anger building, both with me and with himself. As I later discovered, he knew he should drop the subject, knew he was only lacerating himself by dwelling on it, but yet he couldn't help it. It spoiled things for him, this knowledge that I had shared myself with others, fearing I enjoyed them more than him. But this was Alec, and this was the old green-eyed monster. It works on old insecurities, on fears embedded deep in the past, in the youthful times when patterns of need and desire are forming.

When I returned dripping and shaking, and removed my cap so that my hair still clung to my head, I felt suddenly ugly, conscious of my prominent ears, normally covered with thick curly hair; a family legacy. Cass reckoned we all 'looked like taxis with the doors open'. As I picked up my towel and began to dry myself, he looked up. 'I'm sorry,' he said, 'It's none of my business.'

'I didn't say that, and I'm not wanting to hide anything from you. Of course it's your business, if it's anybody's business apart from mine. That's why I told you about Clarrie, and told you that I've had other affairs. I didn't want any secrets between us.'

'I know. You told me. But sometimes I wish you hadn't.'

'Clarrie was awful. He was mean, and dishonest, and if you want to know, the sex between us was hateful.'

Even if this pleased Alec, yet he still was not happy, and would not relent. It was the thought of me with someone else. His anger now turned into a sulk, and it was a sulk that lasted all the rest of the day. All the way back to the hotel he hardly said a word. He said he didn't want any lunch, so I ordered a sandwich and ate it in the hotel garden alone, and afterwards went back to the room for a nap. He was there, reading the paper, but still didn't speak. This lasted through the afternoon and evening, all through dinner. We slept in the double bed facing away from each other, and even my quiet weeping did not bring him round. He was punishing me, that was the only conclusion I could draw. He was still silent in the morning, as we moved around each other to use the bathroom, dress, and ready ourselves to go to breakfast. I thought I would go crazy if he kept it up, and finally it was only the news in the morning paper that enabled us to break the ice. German troops had invaded Poland, and the papers were full of speculation about the implications for a general War. He sparked up at the news, which had the effect of suddenly changing his whole mood. At the breakfast table in the hotel dining room he wanted to talk about it, particularly the whole matter of Australian involvement. 'Some of us might have to front up for service,' he said, with a touch of optimism. I think this was the first time Alec gave any serious thought to joining up. In a few months, when Australian troops were being shipped overseas, he was to take the whole question even more seriously.

The marriage limped along over the following months, with me making an effort to give it a chance. We found a little terrace in Footscray from where he could catch the tram to work, and which was convenient for me to visit my parents in Williamstown. I tried to keep him happy, but his moods would always come and go, and I eventually saw that he was never going to change, and that his malaise had nothing to do with me and everything to do with the way he felt about himself.

And then came the War, and in early 1942 Alec joined up. He'd been itching to do it ever since he listened to the Prime Minister's announcement supporting Britain. At last he would have the chance to be part of the world of men. Blokes at work had joined up, even some of the women had left office work to train in the services. He had been nervous of being rejected because of his asthma, but the medical examination cleared him, and he was accepted. It was a great disappointment to him when he was posted to the Ordnance Corps, and given the purely clerical job of keeping records of the movement of parked artillery. At first he believed that his unit was to be sent to the Middle East, where he was assured by some of the other fellows that they would see 'plenty of action'. But with fears for Australia now the main concern, they ended up spending the War in Townsville. It meant that Alec could get down to Melbourne for his leave, and at first he would stay with me in Footscray, but with the feeling between us all but lost, and our sexual activity little more than duty – on my part anyway – he was eventually persuaded to base himself at Camberwell with Ivy.

We never lived together after that. He wrote letters telling me of his life in the army, which despite what seemed to me a very soft and dreary cop, he had come to love. Occasionally I answered them, but I was never able to return his hopes for a reconciliation. After the War he joined the CMF, dressing up and playing at soldiers with similarly dedicated, or lonely, mates. I heard that he rose through the ranks and became an officer. We didn't do anything about a divorce until it became necessary. That was initiated by me in the late 1940s when I met the real love of my life, a story that doesn't belong here. Alec was resisting up until then, hoping we'd get back together. But once it became evident that this would never happen, he launched himself into a series of marriages – not affairs, which in those days tended to give even the man something of a soiled reputation – but the full nuptial leap. Three times he married between the late 1940s and 1970s, and each one of them a disaster, though to be fair, the one after me – Joyce – ended because she died from cancer, and they had a daughter. But they weren't happy even so, and the two subsequent marriages, which produced three more children in total, were dismal failures, ending in divorce. The pattern was plain enough to anyone: he was impossible to live with, but attractive enough to take to bed. And his attitude to women was itself a mixture of hot and cold: passionate need, turning to corrosive jealousy. As I said at the beginning, I can't fathom how I ever succumbed.

Poems

Aubade

for Joy and Stuart: Vale

Waking, staring at the wall
I await your stir and roll;

my hand slips under your top,
yours moves and rests in my lap:

geriatric tries at sex
tending to become burlesque,

instead I rise to entertain
the indifferent porcelain;

a modest fart (not unheard)
and I depart kitchenward

to make your morning pekoe,
(a brew too pissing weak, oh

how you can drink that fly's pee
without whisky confounds me).

Rattling with each trembling step,
the cup and I avoid mishap

till placed within your grateful
purview; then that delightful

smile that might suggest the drawn
drapes sun-flooding-in the dawn.

On the Highway

The asphalt rushes up and under,
eager to meet our headlong plunge;
along the margins of vision
variations of green sweep by
window-tilted in reflections at once forgotten.
How many sweet-sucking, jazz-rhythmed hours
must pass until the groin pain
finally gets its way
and we change places, she and I?

It used to be that the journey was broken
by the greeting of each small town,
where deserted streets wide as the Murray
bear night-time mainies and full donuts
metres short of both gutters.
You could have a pee and a pie, or if
you were the organised type, unwrap
your sandwich and open the thermos
in the local Rotary-funded park,
read the plaque under the bronze anzac,
and watch the squealing sprites on the swings.
But now only the board signs mark their way,
mere names and directions:
exit to Kilmore, Seymour, Euroa, Violet Town,
Wangaratta' or Sweetwater Creek for that matter;
what are they like any more, those towns?
Some of them do still thrive; their tenor
changed by an injection of fresh blood,
refugees looking for a new life
opening main road cafes

and reviving local canneries.
This way the town young
find unexpected lovers and wives,
their torn parents troubled by the Other,
but grateful they aren't leaving for the city,
and for the chance of sitting
A swart new grandchild.
This way the town will again draw
the curious traveller, and grow.

Away from the big freeway,
dodging pot-holes, making tight curves,
you get a taste of the silent life
in the peeling farmhouses,
haysheds falling
to earth in freeze-frame
self-demolition. Time here
snails into the future,
the change in tree clumps and
stretches of raffish grass so slow
the landscape looks the same as last year,
but isn't. The only movement you see
is the wind-shadows rippling
the surface of paddocks.
When you make that last stretch
to your destination, it is only then
that the tiredness hits. You
take the luggage out
of the bug-spattered car,
and standing on the firm ground feel strange,
your head dizzy with the ghost of movement,
your brain enacting the vestige of motion,

your heart dropping with a hint
of sadness that the journey is over.
Wherever it is you were going, you are there,
and part of you wishes you were not.

NB. 'Mainies' are what country youths call driving up and down the
main street of their small town at night. 'Donuts' are making a circle on
the road with your tyres as the rear wheels spin fast.

Ghost Town

To Jo

That first week of romance
wanting to share a personal secret
you led me to a deserted place
in the old goldfields
of Castlemaine,
where dry buildings,
sunlit in grey weatherboard,
were being sucked back into the earth;
a rusting mine-winch half sunk in a grass knoll,
a broken sieve and bottomless buckets
attended the burial.
The only gold now, daffodils
in scattered clumps, and nodding snowdrops,
detonated from the earth
in frozen green explosions,
waited upon our arrival.
In this sad, vacant community
even the ghosts were missing,
except that a light breeze playing
across the stumpy eucalypts
made the leaves shimmer
like grey-green costumes
set upon a haunt.

This was your home turf
where you breathed-in memories
like an old smoker
and it entered the blood and fed
your heart and face and perfect legs,

leapt the sinews and synapses of your frame,
till it shaped your thought -
A historian's thought,
though bookless and unwritten.

Twilit City 1958

Empty offices, jangling phones ignored, entry doors locked;
typists and clerks hurriedly dispersed to crowded trains and trams;

in the streets lone stragglers are staying on for an evening class
against the future, or guiltily for an assignation.

The city's engine slows after hours of regular turbulence.
From the post office steps you look down on the derelict man,

windblown trash circling his crusty trousers, bent on his endless
sort through the bins, hopeful of a pristine sandwich or half a pie;

permanence is an illusion; you fear a huge abyss might open,
swallow buildings, streets, and these unlucky few, including you.

The angled sun glints on the metal tramlines, casts long
shadows along Bourke Street, presaging its fall behind the row

of buildings mounted on the western rise – McCall's bookshop,
a State bank, McEwans hardware, Coles & Garrard the optician.

All quiet, except for the howl of a tram coasting along Elizabeth
street and the paperboy's strangled cries echoing from the corner.

Soon the theatres will start, the crowds re-emerge. Now drifters
vanish into restaurants opening their doors, disgorged from pubs
closing theirs.

You eat in a Bistro from the past – in a basement in Little Collins,
Italian. You like its dim lighting, its bentwood chairs, its
waiters in white aprons, and the pleasant aroma of coffee and fish.

You eat fresh ciabatta with ravioli bolognese topped with parmesan,
which your mother did not know. While you're eating you wonder
where you'll be in thirty years' time.

You emerge from the shadows up the steps into the street, surprised
to find the bright city still there, but busier, noisier, more colour.

Unsure, you think you might be happy, but the canopy of sky above
is now stained by the ink-leaching dark, empty of stars. Empty.

Travelogue

Connemara hilltop view:
spread of fields and farms
whispers in my ear, 'Home'.

Track up to Momotombo
pink embers wink through grey ash
between wisps of hot smoke.

Indians at Delhi seminars,
synergistic professionals,
especially the women.

The black widows of Chania scowl from doorways,
but say 'Kalimera' and they explode
in gap-toothed smiles.

Near death in Sri Lanka, you are
saved by a mystery potion from
the local medicine man.

The Nuka Hiva bus driver has feet
as large as snow-shoes; her ancestors
almost ate Herman Melville.

The foreigner in a Beijing bathhouse
can be happy that his average-size todger
is likely bigger than anyone else's.

The locals of Papeete simmer with resentment
at French colonial rule that ignores them
or sells them to tourists.

Cancun gets so hot in summer
the outdoor pools are
warmer than the swimmers.

The attendants in the Paris Zoo poked the monkeys
with long staffs; we threatened the same
to the attendants.

A Vence family restaurant; father spruiks; son waits on tables;
from the kitchen mother brings a tray of roast potatoes:
'How many would you like?' she smiles.

Bike-riding and sex are skills for life, they say;
in Cambodia you kept falling off, were dinked home.
In bed you kept your balance.

The holograph in the Shanghai museum shows
tiny replicas of families interacting at home,
real people shrunk down to children's toys.

Cars at Santa Barbara intersections politely take turns
to cross; each respects the order, none reneges.
A socialist ideal.

In the San Francisco B&B all guests appear at breakfast,
tell their stories while everyone listens.
A democratic ideal.

Picasso's 'Guernica' in Madrid demolishes the split
between art and propaganda;
modernism's great anti-war poster.

On the Las Vegas 'Strip' two galleons engage in a sea-battle;
we sleep the night in the car park for customers
of the 'Treasure Island' casino.

Through a Prague cafe window the medieval figure of Death
strikes the hour on the Astronomical clock; overlooking the square
is Franz Kafka's old apartment.

The Cu Chi tunnels in Vietnam have 18 inch manholes;
families lived there for years like rats, hiding
from Australian soldiers.

The shower in the Delhi guest house has water pipes,
not connected to any water supply.
There is a tap and bucket.

The bomb-damaged *pension* in Belgrade;
through the bedroom window the full moon reflects in the river;
husky with love, you whisper, 'The Danube'.

A pair of wedge-tailed eagles circle over a hill in Alice Springs;
in turn male and female noiselessly swoop to feed
from the ranger's hand.

Fukuoka airport; a Japanese man defers to us at the escalator;
from a phone box his violent shouts fill the building with terror;
at his wife?

Dawn light filters through our Chania bedroom;
the regular slapping from below is of fishermen
beating octopus against the harbour wall.

The boat we sat in glided on the Danube, on the right bank Buda's
grand elevation, on the left Pest's deer-coloured parliament,
floating in tranquil overconfidence. You felt like a queen.

The bookshop in Broome run by a woman who loves literature.
Her stock is surprising in range and quality,
and she will buy your second-hand discards.

The empty church of Saint Francis in Cochin,
where in 1524 Vasco da Gama prayed,
died on Christmas eve, and was buried.

Small Mercies

So blindly striving to complete the work
constructing me, nudging the throng apart,
the seed might easily have missed its mark.

Fate did dictate the path ahead seemed stark,
but I *felt* the way, guessing dross from art,
so blindly striving to complete the work.

Same with girls: throwing a blonde for a dark,
I almost foundered after that bad start;
the seed might easily have missed its mark.

Then came the friend's wrong but well-meant remark
that I must find myself in books; the heart
so blindly striving to complete the work,

threatened itself with making life a lark,
and, risking the price for being unalert,
the seed might easily have missed its mark.

Yes, I should have felt more pain, let the spark
attack the bone so deeply that it hurt;
but blindly striving to complete the work
the seed might easily have missed its mark.

Keeping Time

They sit together on a garden seat
                    the old man and the cat;
     a Haydn trio airs
                from the house.
Grey whiskers glint
                in the sun,
      oversized ears listen,
                narrowed eyes
 look, but comprehend?
     It is the world in the head matters,
not the passengers in
                the passing
                        car.
The honey-eater on the branch
                adds a third movement:
Its fall
       from twig
              to flower
catches
      the eye of man and cat,
                watching in hope.
Each of this trio lives
              at a certain tempo:
Andante, Adagio, Presto.
        The cat is poised,
      the old man slow,
      the bird quick.

Tutorial on Pope

What walls between them and the past

On their knees the words
collapse into specks of ash

I half turn in my chair;
through the window the sky is crushing
the suburbs into a flat carpet

How to begin? Biography?
The little monkey was kicked by a cow,
grew up crippled and spiteful
and compensated with bonny verse?

Context? Underprivilege was rife;
the constant problem of disposing
of excrement?
(they deem this irrelevant)

Criticism? Only an oxymoron
could confuse syllepsis
with zeugma?

What walls between myself and the past
and the present

I want them to see anger
the courage of a mind with its back
up against history
nothing in his gun but words

Isolation Cell, Port Arthur, 1850

The isolation cell at Port Arthur prison, created in 1849, totally deprived the prisoner of light and sound for anything between one and three months at a stretch. Prisoners frequently emerged mentally impaired.

What can be known in this black,
but the earth underfoot, the walls I touch?
My fingers brush crumbling skin
tenderly
as it were the body of a dead lover.

These coat buttons,
plucked, are useless
as a snowman's eyes;
blindly strewn about the cell,
they wait for redemption
by my saviour hands.

Pulsing sheath, warm in my loins,
and comrade cloth, my only friends.
I would die, but lack the means.
I would penetrate these yard-thick walls
with memories – the white cry of gull,
green feel of grass, blue breath of sky,
whiff of something
whose name I no longer know
over the bucketful of stink
somewhere behind me,
but recall is weak without clues;
there are no clues.
Besides, the shit spoils everything.

Here no name, no face, no voice;
nothing but the almost-imagined,
almost-alive, almost-dead. Move,
resist, go on, a heartbeat from those graves
somewhere across the bay.

Again I scatter the buttons to the void,
Listen, catch their rattle,
begin the quest once more,
tentative fingers brailling the uncanny,
till eight-in-hand, in triumph
I clutch them to my breast, affirmed,
unspeaking,
the story unfinished finished.

Road Kill

In their dress sense crows show
their humours to be in perfect
                    balance;
            sloping away from
the carcass
                no sooner than necessary,
fastidiously timing their departure
    to the last
                    moment,
they avoid the speeding grille,
        that would make them
                another's sanguine feast.
Princes of the phlegmatic,
        they stay near their
                    repast,
knowing the cars are ephemeral
                    interruptions, mere
drop-ins
                that don't belong
        and will soon pass;
but their dark cry is a
                    wild burst of
        choler hurled at the sky
                    from a dead branch,
    then the mock-melancholy fade
and echo
                to a hollow silence;
what other garb could they wear
                    but funereal black?

In Memoriam

Robert Laurence Haberfield

Making friends has not been my greatest trick
through the years ; a few men, fewer women,
desire being a problem, either surfeit
or paucity; the fault lies in the dick
I could say, but that is the bad workman
blaming the tool. Often my sins have been
about meanness of spirit, the too-strict
heart finding defects in decent human
endeavour, desiring others' defeat.
Ergo, friendships came few and far between.

My closeness to those few men, I will say,
has been something else again. Part cobbers,
talking of cricket, football, men's fashion,
or politics, the mind-drug of the day,
part rivals, each boasting of our clobber,
making sure we exacted due respect.
Yet we were always critical, sought a way
to make a point, share an insight of a
hitherto unobserved thing, with a passion
only the artist in us can expect.

Your example showed me the rightness of this;
It came to you naturally, your mixed state
of intensity and calm self-possession.
There was a darkness one could easily miss
unless one took time to interrogate
the pain that lurked in those hungry brown eyes.
I knew that pain to stem from the abyss
of a young father's death, a mother's hate
of self when facing lifelong destitution.
We had the same lost loves; ours were shared ties.

When first we met, young in choco-soldier gear,
our attraction was perhaps the response
of wound-to-wound as much as smile-to-smile.
Anyway, you showed me never to fear
to act on instinct, despite looking a ponce
in the eyes of the pharisaic herd.
Be a snob, be remote; what should we care?
Reject the ordinary, mere common sense,
be true to your love of surprise and style,
you said; those philistines would praise a turd.

So, hanging together, you taught me to feel,
to see and, above all, preserve wonder.
You led me through my first gallery visit
when we came upon that Monet, *Vétheuil,*
and you exclaimed 'It's so *warm*!' There, under
your spell, I could actually feel the heat
across the gleaming Seine like it was real;
an education with no agenda.
With music, you taught me the requisite
open heart and mind, from Bach to Basin Street.

My instincts were defensive, raised in fear
of someone thinking I was two-plank thick;
yet I was never content with the norm.
The thing I learned from you was that to hear,
see, or feel something new would never wreck
my fragile self, but likely make it tough.
Art, at its most aggressive, can surely tear
you open, or maybe make you feel sick
at times, but it cannot permanently harm.
The shock does pass, the wounds heal soon enough.

I knew the wondrous journeys of your art
were decent aristocratic reserve,
Yet I chose to politicize myself,
which long drove a wedge that kept us apart.
You then suffered a strange failure of nerve,
gave in to the dollar and the bottle,
till death or desperation could jump-start
your quest for a wise, balanced way to live.
For years you vanished to a spiritual self
and your work turned, I thought, sentimental.

I say this now, having since understood
that what looked like *schlock* to the biased eye
were in fact crackingly executed
icons of true belief, no earthly good
to the aesthete, collector or gallery.
And not much good to me, I should confess,
except in this single sense, that I could
see, in all your strokes, the continuity
from the early to the last work was rooted
in you, Bob, the self no code could suppress.

It took a level of intimacy
peculiar to close friends to grasp as much;
you may have seen me, in my work, in quite
the same way; I understood you, and you me.
But for all our care, differences that touch
on life's small accidents and chance meetings
remained, and our paths moved separately,
determined by the ties that bind, and such.
We were like two halves seeking to unite
but finding contact never more than fleeting.

The dazzling arabesque of your progress
was a star seen only by the few who
were lucky to be awake at that moment.
It was my privilege to be sleepless
and witness the sheer talent that blessed you.
Despite the distance, our last years were bliss;
we facetimed, skyped, phoned, even stood the stress
of flights to each other's home, because we knew
we needed that last gesture of content
to clinch the friendship lovers choose to miss.

Wishful Thought

One day the best thing in the world occurred:
everyone's deepest secrets became known.
Lies broke from dark cells, and, sentenced by word,
their deceit was now out there to be shown
full of bad conscience, cheats proclaimed
themselves open now to common sight.
Rancid basements where children had been maimed
and jailed, were flooded now with candid light,
repugnant men who kept them forced to face
their hateful actions in full public gaze.
Out they came, these secrets of our sleazy race
long itched and frigged, in a penitent craze.
The greed driving rich and poor to fraud and scam
leaked out for all to see, and hold in shame.

Thus lies became the truth, and hidden sins
became the tales that educate and warn;
the one about the man who always wins
converted to a work of love reborn.

The Refinery Across Corio Bay

Distance works magic: a note
of measure between fact and eye,
when either too close or too remote,
makes humans monstrous or puny.

Gazed-at over river or sea,
'more fair' only shows sublime
if you can't hear the beggar's plea,
or see the carcass in the river slime.

On these lovely sunlit mornings
we may fall to risky spells
when, aching with Cavafy's longings,
we imagine Alexandrian walls,
ivory mansions trimming the Corniche,
across the bay, within eye's reach.

Yet by noon, when the mist has burned,
and the sun has opened up the angle,
the scene is clear and brazenly zoomed:
now raucous zinc bellies dangle
skeleton arms and legs and whang
their inorganic toxic racket,
and we know the whole packet
lies – a swindling kilometer long.

Four Human States

Excitement

Of the four stem states of human feeling
excitement is the most ephemeral.
We may be joyful, angry or fearful
but these quickly reach a point of failing.
So we embark upon the act of love,
fall to fighting with our galling neighbour,
or fear the presence of an invader,
until the moment passes and we move
into a different state. For instance, pain
is excitement of a very special kind
but it inevitably subsides we find,
or ceases and begins its thrust again;
try to extend excitement's natural span
and it will by diversion thwart the plan.

Contentment

Contentment is often misunderstood;
it is not satisfaction, though might stretch
in some circumstances to provide such.
Nor is it indifference, though easily could
descend to it. It really is that state
of moderated living in which we
do our daily tasks – walk, drive, watch tv
socialise, water the garden, or eat,
performed not intensely, but as routines,
time-filling things automatically done,
not weighted down in gloom, nor buoyed in fun,
but more like prolonged and tempered daydreams.
Most time is in contentment's daily peace;
the contract from which we never seek release.

Grief

Invasive, severer than contentment,
absorbing each of us at some stage, grief
insists we recognize its role as chief
of states, far more potent than excitement,
more oceanic than depression (yet
it might include this); grief is not ill-health
but a perception about life itself.
Once felt, it can't be improved or reset.
Grief instils the conviction that each day
is an ordeal of loss, waste its offshoot:
lost chances, strength, beauty, lost childhood, youth,
above all lost time, our lives leaching away.
Armed with this inexorable logic
grief makes life's mode inherently tragic.

Love

Conventionally, this we tell ourselves,
is our saving grace; all-conquering, brave,
defiant in the face of despair, love
would seek to redeem the crime it resolves.
But ancient Greeks believed it a disease;
Freud said it wants what it wants when it wants;
I try to search my heart for love's true sense
but find only variance; a spring breeze,
balmy in the right moment, cold the next;
hot fingering of flesh, or mere idea;
thought only for self, to fend off the fear
of death, yet capable on small pretext
of giving even this one treasured life
to ease another's pain or make them safe.

An Early Leaver

Never has she left the house with such frequent purpose:
she eats less, dresses young, hides the birth-scars
with skill, and litters the rooms with arrogant books.

In classes she talks wastefully, but with the force
of a decade of gagging; her younger colleagues defer.
This is her second beginning, no mistakes this time.

Her husband does not understand; where did he go wrong?
He gave her everything he could – his love, his children,
and now she talks to him of Engels or Jonathan Swift.

He makes an effort to keep her on the right path
by placing a television set in every room,
but she won't stop her damn writing in the kitchen.

She recoils at night from love:
twenty years of that grind
has shaken her dry.

A fresh lust stirs in its place,
engorges words, germinates scruples,
breeds toddling essays.

Each day she drives home in guilt;
already she teaches her heart self-defence
and how to pass the hours alone.

Magpie

For Madeleine, Emma, Anya and Geordi

These past three days in the garden,
a magpie has waited to greet me;
he won't fly away, or maybe he can't,
but it's clear he's not frightened to meet me.

When I step outside he comes running
like a small armless child to its mother;
a gleam in his eye and head on one side,
as if putting some question or other.

His tail feathers spiky and shaggy,
his black head all scarred from a fight,
his dress-sense is ruffled, and baggy,
it looks like he's stayed up all night.

His hunger for meat is ferocious;
he quickly scoffs cold bolognaise,
a rissole or sausage or ham off the bone ;
you'd swear he'd not eaten for days.

It's obvious now he's a young'un
and doesn't know much about life;
his screeches and squeals are disturbing
like a blackboard that's scraped with a knife!
He's singing right now at the sunset,
or perhaps he is calling a mate.

Whatever the reason it doesn't seem right
to be all on his own 'cos his family took flight
and headed for Queenscliff one dark moonlit night,
and left him to me, as his fate.

Tabatha

for David Galloway

We hadn't seen her all day;
by eight I began to worry.
It was a winter's bitch of a night,
with a sharp wind and needles of rain
driving up between the house and fence.

The torchlight found her crouching
in the lee of a low wall; if she'd been
asking to come in, the howl of the wind
had drowned her cries. But then again,
she might not have wanted to bother
the world with her pain.

Racked by shivers,
her tight-knotted huddle her one defence
against the piercing cold and arrows of fire,
her eyes brimming, not with self-pity,
she waged a passionate resistance.

Despite my careful lifting, a small cry
escaped her control. Placed
next to the heater, she fixed me with
steady green eyes. Gratitude? Perhaps.
An exchange of understanding ? Yes.

Small-bodied, neatly marked tabby-and-white,
a devoted member of the family for fifteen years,
she would emulate our better human traits:
loyalty; affection; the tidiness that considers others.
Mornings she walked the children halfway to school,
protecting them like they were her kittens.

She would chase off the neighbour's idiot dog
and could force a battle-scarred tom
to slink off in fear just by staring it down.
And yet she purred like a diesel on a steady lap,
and slept with the children to share their dreams.

Next day at the vet's, she waited more patiently
than we as the queue snailed through the morning.
On the table, his practised hands quickly felt the lump.
After the necessary words, everyone knew
what must happen. Gently held while the needle went in,
she looked into our faces secure in the faith
that her gods were with her, then was still.

After Yabbies

For Ray

This little creek
between streets
curtained in green
willow boughs
was flowered
with patient,
heartless
boys.

Yesterday's lamb
offcut
on a lure of twine
lowered with care
drawn to the surface
with surgical poise
until the flip of antenna
was taken between
forefinger and thumb,
blue claws waving
semaphore
the creature was
lifted and
                dropped
into the bucket,
the festive dream
over.

Kite flying

so

now

people

are busy being

offended and always

at a distance, on phones,

the paper, tv, never face to

face, so busy that surely they

miss the wondrous luck that it

was only theirs not another of

the millions of other striving

spermatozoa, that blindly

found a way to the wall

which it penetrated

and was first in

putting

up the

guard

rail

and

s

t

r

i

k

i

n

g

g

o

l

d

?

The Ballad of Jack Bone

This tale is of Van Diemen's Land in 1844,
when cruelty was exercised on men who broke the Law.
Our eyes turn on the prison, and in each mingy cell
inmates pray for luck to let them die and go to Hell.

The worst repeat offender, Jack shipped from Moreton Bay,
to serve Life at Port Arthur for killing William Day.
Jack Bone was flogged until his back was premium mince;
a murmur never passed his lips, no muscle gave a wince.

But this humiliation altered something in Jack's brain:
he swore they'd never slash his skin nor spill his blood again,
nor break his cold defiance, nor bring his spirit down
with 'cat' or with surveillance, or any torture known.

The moon shines on Port Arthur, as it is bound to do;
and Jack determines an escape, to join another two.
Three nights ago they bolted in a stolen prison skiff,
and Jack has vowed to follow them when chance gives him a sniff.

The prison guards are watching, watching day and night;
they watch his every movement, watch his every bite.
They overhear his breathing, and listen to his farts;
try to catch his thinking, and when his dreaming starts.

But Jack Bone the rebel knows just how to choose his time,
to strike the very moment when his strength is at its prime.
The word of how to slip the heavy irons passes round,
and Jack well knows the secret, soon has both his legs unbound;
and before the guards can know it, with one astounding leap,
he clears the prison ramparts, lands upon his feet.

Into the bush he scampers, bound for Eaglehawk Neck,
where lines of guards could shoot him, or vicious dogs attack.
But Jack knows how to vanish, slip past their raking lines
by mimicking a wallaby, or covering up the signs

his stealthy movement leaves, or like the Frogmouth sly,
perching in the tree tops, quite hidden from the eye.
The Bush becomes his cover, hides his every track;
imagination turns his mind to imitation black.

And preservation forces-in the knowledge to transcend
the limits of the likely, and the rules of matter bend.
(For the alien bush's mystery is to the native black
as plain as water to a fish, its maze, an almanac).

So legend gives Jack magic power well beyond the norm;
the spirit of the moment transmogrifies his form:
a guard might catch a glimmer, urge on his straining dog,
but finds the apparition now a 'blackboy', now a log.

The troopers cannot catch him, he finds a passage through,
and by that very evening Jack has found the other two.
They hunker down together, O'Driscoll, Jack and Hyde,
afraid to light a fire, lest the fire should be espied.

O'Driscoll's talk is cheerful, he thinks his freedom's won,
but Hyde is full of terror, convinced his life is done;
yet Jack gives in to neither, escape his only thought,
'My life', he swears to heaven, 'will expensively be bought'.

The night is clear as crystal and cold as arctic sleet;
they make a bed of gum leaves, join bodies to make heat.
All night they lie uneasy, imagining their lot,
each sough of tree a pant of dog, each snapping twig a shot.

So sick with cold and hunger, exhausted and downcast,
in fitful sleep their nightmares revoke their cruel past;
Hyde revels in his suffering, O'Driscoll comes to hate
his silly thoughts of freedom, and Jack accepts his fate.
But such character reversals alas have come too late
For the die is cast, and no man can thwart nature's designate.

The dawn sun rises weakly within the silver bush,
The magpie sings her lyric cry to pierce the misty hush;
the limbs begin their stirring, damp from the drifting fog,
O'Driscoll lies in Jack's embrace, moves not a limb, nor eyes, nor face,
of breath or sound gives not a trace, dead as a poisoned dog.

'He had the dreaded madness,' says Hyde, 'that's why he laughed
when things were at their damndest, his talk went utter daft.'
'His heart gave out,' Jack mumbles, 'He couldn't take the strain',
and drags the lifeless body that now lies beyond pain
into a hidden gully, where time and Tassie weather
will guarantee O'Driscoll's body disappears forever.
'We must go on,' Jack urges, 'we have to make the Neck
before the troopers have a chance to get formations back.'

Heedless of the mounting heat the desperate convicts push
through scrub and gumtree forest and dense Tasmanian bush,
until they reach a clearing, not far to where they strive,
and Hyde attests he needs a rest if he's to stay alive.

'To buggery with that,' Jack Bone responds, and plunges on,
but the weaker man collapses on his knees, his spirit gone.
'Keep going Jack,' he mutters, 'I'm done for, that's a fact.'
and face-down in the clearing – falls, with no strength left to act.

Through bush as thick as treacle Jack presses on ahead,
his prison garb in tatters, his hopeless shoes in shreds,
'Til finally the distant sound of – wait on, could it be –
the crash of waves, the foaming white, the ever-roiling sea?

And through the trees the golden sand like honeyed land appears,
And silent joy within his heart bursts out in crazy cheers:
'Your freedom's won, your struggle's done,
You've reached the Neck, you devil's son,
they'll die before they take Jack Bone!'
But fate has new ideas:

Out from behind a spill of rocks the arméd troops emerge,
while over at his rearward three more boys in blue converge,
then stalking from within the bush more guards with guns in hand
surround him all, and closing in they order Jack to 'Stand!'
He freezes, taken unawares, his eyes dart round in fear;
no way of breaking through their lines, no exit would appear
to offer any hope of Jack reversing such bad luck.
'We've got him now,' the sergeant calls, 'surrender Bone, you fuck!'

In desperate thought Jack wonders if he'd make it to the sea,
run helter-skelter through their lines and end up dead, or free;
but the thing that he'd neglected in his care for life and limb:
In all his thirty-seven years – he'd never learned to swim!

In any case he knows he'd never make it to the sea,
they'd have him full of bullet holes before he counted three;
his only chance is back into the bush from where he'd been
and so, retreating stealthily, he merges with the green;

the bristly mass of native shrub and thicket holds him tight;
the saltbush and the wattle camouflages him from sight.
The stubborn troopers won't give up, they want his vicious hide;
their straining dogs can smell him, and a man's stink never lied.

They push on ever closer, in belief they've got their man,
yet when they reach the clearing Jack has disappeared again.
They miss him at ground zero, because they cannot know
he's climbed a soaring eucalypt, obscured from view below;

And there the dogs can't get him, though they sense he's gone up high
where the foliage and the branches partly shield him from the eye.
And this creates a stalemate between escape and pursuit;
no way presents itself to hunt, no target there to shoot.

The thwarted troops are wearied, they lie and sit and think;
they take to their tobacco, or from canteens a cool drink;
the sergeant takes his cap and wipes it on his sweating brow,
'It's growing dark,' he mutters, 'we'll never see him now';

'We'll get him yet,' a corporal says, 'with a hail of musket ball,
we'll riddle every branch and leaf to make the bastard fall!'
The sergeant gives the order: round on pitiless round
blasts the evening twilight with its fearful, lethal sound.

Every living creature, from the screeching cockatoo
to the tiger and the devil, and the Tassie kangaroo
panics at the noise of death, and scatters where it can;
every living creature – except one defiant man.

And does he go on living? Or does his body fall?
for certain the expected crash does not take place at all;
and when the sergeant's order comes at last to 'cease your fire!,'
Jack Bone has not descended, and the corporal made a liar.

'Chop down the bloody tree then,' the angry sergeant cries,
'One way or another I will have him, damn his eyes!'
An axe is brought, a watch is kept for any move up top,
then with groan and crash almighty the old tree completes its drop.

They search among the foliage, green and thick upon the ground,
they prod it and they poke it, but no body can be found;
it's clear to each observer that the tree was felled in vain,
and Jack Bone the convict has escaped them once again.

And now the weakened sun draws down the dusky shades of night,
and tree, and bush and clearing nigh impossible to sight;
dejected at their failure, the troops like drifting kine
set out upon the dull trudge back, to the order, 'Fall in line'.

And when the evening grey-thrush sings its age-old lyric trill,
and the sun falls through the wattle and the air is blue and still,
and the happiest human presence in those wild Tasmanian lands
are Palawa aborigines in calm and peaceful bands,

the tales around the campfires told by bushmen to their mates
of cruel Port Arthur punishment, of convicts and their fates,
will mourn the John O'Driscolls and the likes of Kevin Hyde,
and the awful way that many had unfortunately died,
but the one they relish most, and tell their children night and day,
is the story of the bold Jack Bone – the one that got away!

Acknowledgements

'An Early Leaver' first published in *Luna*, Vol.3, 1, 1978; 'A Higher Learning' first published in *Quadrant* magazine, January-February 1979; 'Tutorial on Pope' first published in *The Age*, 23 July 1977.